Alice Smith

A Woman of Mind

A novel. Part 1

Alice Smith

A Woman of Mind
A novel. Part 1

ISBN/EAN: 9783337045555

Printed in Europe, USA, Canada, Australia, Japan

Cover: Foto ©Andreas Hilbeck / pixelio.de

More available books at **www.hansebooks.com**

A WOMAN OF MIND.

𝔄 𝔑𝔬𝔳𝔢𝔩.

BY

MRS. ADOLPHE SMITH,

AUTHOR OF "LOVE WITHOUT WINGS."

IN THREE VOLUMES.

VOL. I.

LONDON:

SAMPSON LOW, MARSTON, SEARLE & RIVINGTON,

CROWN BUILDINGS, 188, FLEET STREET.

1879.

LONDON:
PRINTED BY WILLIAM CLOWES AND SONS,
STAMFORD STREET AND CHARING CROSS.

A WOMAN OF MIND.

CHAPTER I.

THE breakfast-bell had rung at Clevedon House, and the party had gradually assembled in the spacious breakfast-room. Lady Leveson and her daughter were at the window, admiring, or professing to admire, the fine expanse of green land and blue sky stretched before them; Gilbert Jocelyn was indulging in a scarcely disguised yawn by the mantel-piece; and Admiral and Mrs. Clevedon were watching the door with evident anxiety, not unmixed with displeasure.

"Where can Silvia be?" murmured Mrs. Clevedon, glancing deprecatingly at Lady Leveson.

"She is really incorrigible," said the admiral, angrily; and he added, turning to the servant who stood beside him with the letter-bag, "Johnson, ring the breakfast-bell again. Miss Clevedon cannot have heard."

While the house was yet echoing to the sound of the peal, Mrs. Clevedon, who had glanced out of the window, exclaimed, "She is coming. She was in the grounds, you see."

"Who can that be with her?" said the admiral, following his wife's eyes, and seeing that his daughter was not alone.

"It is one of the maids, I should think," hazarded Lady Leveson.

Here Mrs. Clevedon sighed deeply, and said confidentially to her guest, "My daughter has picked up some such very odd ideas, you know, on social matters. I suppose they come from books; she has read extensively and indiscriminately. Her father and I are quite distressed to find that she is developing into a politician, and positively into a regular Radical!" Here Lady Leveson drew involuntarily nearer to her daughter, as if to shield her from the contamination of the very word, and smiled somewhat contemptuously as Mrs. Clevedon continued: "The admiral was always as sound and thorough a Tory as his father before him, and I haven't a drop of anything but the purest Tory blood in my veins; but, in spite of this, Silvia's ideas are totally opposed to ours, on every point."

Gilbert Jocelyn had advanced leisurely to the group by the window, while Mrs. Clevedon was speaking, and he now exclaimed, as Miss Clevedon walked slowly up the broad path towards the house, talking earnestly to the girl at her side, "Radical or not, she's deucedly handsome."

"Yes, yes, she's handsome enough," muttered the admiral, testily; "but I wish she were more practicable."

And Lady Leveson smiled, while her daughter flushed and pouted at the younger man's ingenuous remark.

She was, undeniably, excessively hand-

some; the face and style were not cal-
culated to please every one, but few
could refuse to acknowledge that she
possessed great and striking beauty. And
even Lady Leveson and her daughter,
who assuredly looked with small favour
on Miss Clevedon's personal gifts, could
not but own, as they watched her, that
she might be to some persons' tastes.
It was a serious, thoughtful face that
was turned to the attentive maid—a face
full of intellect and energy and feeling;
and you felt, as you marked its handsome
features and earnest expression, that it
belonged to a woman above the ordinary
feminine level, a woman whom to know
might be "a liberal education."

"She has altered greatly," observed
Gilbert Jocelyn to Mrs. Clevedon. "I

did not see it as much last night as I do now. The daylight shows her up better."

"Yes; she has altered in every way," Mrs. Clevedon answered, with something like a sigh. "She grows more and more strange, and whimsical, and peculiar, day by day."

"She always bid fair to be odd and irregular," laughed Gilbert Jocelyn. "I remember I used to think her a bit of a genius in her way."

"I am very sorry that I am late, father," said Silvia, entering the room at that moment, and advancing towards the group of persons by the window. "Pray excuse my apparent rudeness, Lady Leveson and Miss Leveson," she added, as she shook hands with those ladies, who had looked considerably ruffled at the turn the conversation had been taking before Silvia's appearance.

"How was it that you kept us waiting, Silvia?" asked her father, as the party took their places at the table.

"I did not hear the bell," replied Silvia. "I was interested in talking to Ellen, in giving her some advice."

"It would have been a pity to have interfered with your duties to your maid," said Lady Leveson, with a playful intonation.

"I think it would," replied Silvia, a shade coming over her expressive face; "the girl needed a kind word or two."

Here Gilbert Jocelyn, who had been careful to secure a seat beside Miss Clevedon, broke in: "Why did you not tell me in your letters that you were so

much altered, Silvia? I suppose I may
still call you Silvia?"

The shade that had sobered her countenance a moment before, now gave
way to the brightest of smiles, as she
answered, "Certainly; call me Silvia
still, if it be any satisfaction to you.
It's much more convenient than to wade
through the formality of Miss Clevedon
every time you address me. For my
part, I think it would be far more
sensible if men and women always
addressed each other either by their
Christian names or surnames—that is
to say, if I were to call you Jocelyn,
and you called me Clevedon; or if, on
a more familiar footing, we made it
Gilbert and Silvia. I remember that,
as children, we called each other Gil
and Sil."

"But you are not a child now, Silvia," said her mother, gravely, "and you must try to remember that also."

"Miss Clevedon will always be a child of nature, evidently," said Lady Leveson, icily.

"Thank you," said Silvia, lifting her clear grey eyes to Lady Leveson's face, and smiling. "I take it as a compliment."

Lady Leveson raised her eyebrows, very plainly indicating that she had intended nothing agreeable, and turned to talk with the admiral, resolving, mentally, that she would leave Clevedon House as soon as was consistent with the most elementary rules of good breeding.

"What shall we do when breakfast is over?" said Jocelyn.

"What do you say, Miss Leveson?" said Silvia, glancing across the table at her. "What would you like to do? Will you stroll through the village—such a picturesque village, as pretty, in its way, as anything you can have seen in Switzerland—or shall we ramble into the forest, or have a gallop 'across country'? Which would suit you best?"

"Thank you, I think I would rather not go out this morning," said Miss Leveson, glancing towards her mother for approval. "I have to write one or two letters for mamma, and, also, I don't like walking in the morning much. Of course, I ride in the Row before breakfast in town; but I don't care so much for being out-of-doors in the country."

"You should say as well, my dear

Amy," put in Lady Leveson, "that you are not strong enough for violent exercise. My daughter is very delicate, Miss Clevedon, and is obliged to be very careful. A week or two of galloping across country would stretch her on a bed of sickness."

Silvia bent her head politely, murmuring that she was very sorry to hear it, and the subject was dropped. After breakfast, Lady Leveson and her daughter repaired to their own rooms; Mrs. Clevedon went to the housekeeper's department, for the matutinal confabulation; the admiral took up his letters and papers, saying he was going to look them over in the quiet of the library; and Silvia and Jocelyn were left alone.

"How are you going to amuse me,

Silvia?" asked Jocelyn, by no means displeased at the turn of events. "You know you are bound to look after me, since I am your guest."

"I will do whatever you like," said Silvia, "only let us get out of the house; the very air of the place stifles me."

"Let us take a stroll in the forest, then," said Jocelyn, "and you shall tell me why the air of the house stifles you this breezy, fresh morning."

"I meant the moral air," said Silvia, when, a few moments later, they were walking along a narrow country lane, and Jocelyn had repeated his question. "I have so little sympathy with Lady Leveson and Amy Leveson that their presence checks my freedom of speech, and even of thought, and I find myself constrained and weary and unnatural when I am with them."

"It seemed to me that you were very formal and distant last night," said Jocelyn, "and I thought you were going to insist on obliterating our companionship when we were children."

"I hardly realized you were the same person," said Silvia, smiling. "I have always thought of you as a worrying, teasing boy, given to pulling my hair, throwing snails and caterpillars and beetles at me, filling my hat with innumerable forms of prickly growth, letting off squibs under my window, and burying me in snowballs in winter time; and when I saw you last night in all the inartistic glory of evening dress, and heard all your little courtesies of tone and speech, I could not realize that you were my old playmate. How I wish we were children still! It's a trite saying, but, I think, a true one, that there is nothing like the happiness of childhood."

"But you have not run up and down the scale of happiness, Silvia," said Jocelyn; "you don't know what may be in store for you. How can you tell if your future happiness will or will not outweigh that of your childhood?"

"I don't see how it can," answered Silvia, dreamily. "I can never be as thoughtless and careless as I was in childhood; and directly one begins to think and care seriously for the welfare of others, all entire happiness must be over."

Jocelyn did not answer. He was

slightly taken aback at Silvia's tone, and felt out of his element. The young ladies he met in society were not in the habit of talking in such a strain, and he began to think that these odd ideas might have an unpleasant development occasionally.

They walked along for some time in perfect silence, both occupied with thoughts of each other. The lane had widened to a broad forest path, and the ground was carpeted with well-trodden green grass, and overrun with buzzing flies and gnats. Ferns were growing everywhere, at the foot of every massive tree, in the shade of every stone and mound of earth; and far away, in the distance, the sunlight was seen playing on their waving, feathery masses of green, through the branches of the beech and ash that overshadowed them.

The companions made their way staunchly amid bush and bramble, fern and flower; they climbed a steep hill valiantly, and stood at last on its summit, with a vast expanse of green valley at their feet. Far away, on the horizon, were flecks of white that were devoutly believed to be the tall cliffs of the Isle of Wight, and all around was the marvellous verdure of the magnificent forest. The land rose and fell: here was a steep hill thickly peopled with sturdy oaks, there was a broad stretch of green lawn breaking presently into feathery fern-land; here was a dark band of solemn pines, there were clusters of the brighter beech; but green was everywhere, save immediately at the foot of the hill on which Silvia and Jocelyn were standing, where the breaks in the branches of the trees showed one or two deep-roofed, thatched cottages, almost buried in clambering roses. Not a human creature was to be seen, and the only evidence of the vicinity of humanity was the blue smoke that curled from the chimneys of the dark-roofed, rose-grown homesteads.

"Let us rest here a little," said Jocelyn. "I want to ask you something."

Silvia seated herself instantly on the grass, saying with a smile, "Ask me."

Jocelyn stretched himself lazily at her feet, picked two or three blades of grass, at which he nibbled every now and then, and said, at last, "Is it true,

Silvia, that you are a Radical? Your mother said you were, but I can hardly believe it possible."

"And why should I not be?" asked Silvia, a light in her eyes that had not been there before.

Jocelyn hesitated—he seemed unwilling to speak frankly; and Silvia added, "Speak out, Gilbert. If we are to keep up the friendliness of our childhood, we must keep up its frankness too."

"Well, I was going to say that it is not possible for a lady to be a Radical," said Jocelyn, "for—— "

Here Silvia interrupted him, saying, "I wish you could give me your idea of a Radical?"

"A Radical," said Jocelyn, oracularly, "is a man of the people, as the term

is, who does a vast amount of ranting
and raving about the rights and wrongs
of the people, and who at the very first
opportunity rises above them, if he can,
and leaves them in the lurch. That's
my idea."

"And a just and liberal idea it is,"
said Silvia, with a certain tone of con-
tempt in her voice. "You are a Tory,
I presume, if you are anything," she
added.

"Precisely," replied Jocelyn, lazily.
"I am not enthusiastic in the matter,
and don't really much care about either
party; but still, as you say, if I am
anything, I am bound to be a Tory."

"Well, I will give you my idea of a
Tory," said Silvia, "and then we shall
know how we stand, politically speaking,

in each other's opinions. A Tory is a man of the upper classes, who rants and raves about the enormous intellectual and moral superiority of his own rank, and never does anything that proves it."

Jocelyn burst into a hearty laugh. "I must tell that to North," he said; "he will enjoy it supremely."

"Perhaps North, whoever he may be," said Silvia, "will acknowledge that my definition is correct."

Jocelyn did not speak for a few moments, and when he did, it was to ask, "Where did you learn to be a Radical, Silvia, if you are really so far gone."

"I fancy I must have always been inclined to go so far," said Silvia, looking far away to where the cliffs of the Isle of Wight were shining as she spoke. "I always found myself sympathizing with the wrong people at home. When my mother turned away a kitchen-maid who had been discovered to have stolen a bottle of port for her little brother, who was almost at death's door, and had been ordered port, which his parents could not buy him, my heart was with the thief. When the groom was found tipsy in the stables, and my father had him sent to prison as an example, I was deeply sorry for the poor man, and my father's rigour weighed on my mind for months. When I went to London, before I was presented, I saw so many instances of harshness and injustice, so much misery side by side with the enormous wealth, that the inequality of the present conditions of life struck home to me, and made me profoundly sorry for the sufferings of the people, and anxious to do something to help them to better times."

There was a long silence. Jocelyn looked about him; watched the birds fluttering from twig to twig, from branch to branch of the stately trees; followed with his eyes the slow sailing of a group of vaporous clouds; and finally brought his gaze down to the figure beside him, to the handsome head and stately presence of his old playmate. Then their eyes met, and Silvia said gently—

"You don't understand my ideas, I see, Gilbert. I wondered often, before you came, if we should sympathize in politics, as we did in our childish games —if you would help me through the awkward moments my opinions bring me sometimes, as you invariably helped me in my difficulties as skater, rider, driver."

"Well, you see," said Jocelyn, apologetically, "I have never troubled myself much about politics, about the rights or wrongs of the people or the upper classes, or about anything of that kind, and I have not been among people who did. Of course, I never expected to find you, a woman, and such a young one, interested in them, and from a Radical point of view. You must own that it's unusual."

"Yes, I own that it was unreasonable of me to expect you to share my enthusiasm. And now we will turn homewards, and Amy Leveson shall soothe you with her 'lighter thought.'"

So saying, Silvia started to her feet,

and they retraced their steps, talking and laughing gaily by the way. There was an under-current of disappointment in Silvia's heart, however. She had expected to find a keener intellect, a quicker appreciation, in Gilbert Jocelyn; and when she saw his animation and interest in a warfare of banter with Miss Leveson, she said to herself, " He understands nothing of life but its social graces. I can never make a Radical of him ! "

CHAPTER II.

"Mamma, how long are you going to stay here?" asked Amy Leveson of her mother, the same night, when they had retired and were sitting in the pretty boudoir into which their two bedrooms gave.

"Have you had enough of it already, Amy?" said Lady Leveson, with a laugh.

"I should think I had!" replied Amy, tossing her head, almost angrily. "It's waste of time for me to stop here, you know, mamma. Gilbert Jocelyn will never pay me much attention while that girl is on the scene. If I had him alone, I might bring him to the point one of these days, as you so much wish it; but here I shall do nothing."

"Nonsense, Amy!" said her mother. "Young Jocelyn has known Miss Clevedon all his life; therefore she will not stand in your way. Men never fall in love with girls they have known from childhood. Also, Miss Clevedon is too clever, or pretends to be too clever, for him. Even putting aside the fact that they are old playmates, no man would like a wife who makes him look a fool; and Miss Clevedon made young Jocelyn look a fool once or twice at dinner to-night."

"I'm sure I don't see that she's

clever," said Amy, in a resentful tone. "She talked a great deal, but she was only discussing the games and expeditions she had had with Mr. Jocelyn, and I did not notice anything very remarkable. I wonder how it is that she has been so intimate with Mr. Jocelyn?"

"I can tell you how that happens," said Lady Leveson. "I asked Mrs. Clevedon to-day how it occurred that she allowed her daughter to roam about the forest all the morning alone with a young man, and then she told me that she had always looked on young Jocelyn almost as Miss Clevedon's brother. The boy's father, it appears, was the admiral's dearest friend; they went together through some of those wretched adventures the admiral is so fond of describing.

(How tedious he was this evening! I thought I should have fallen asleep in his face.) Young Jocelyn's mother died at his birth, and when, a year or two afterwards, his father died, he left the care of the child to the admiral. The boy was brought up here, as if in his own home, and left to go to college, and to do the tour of Europe with his tutor, according to his father's wish."

"He is rich, isn't he?" asked Amy, thoughtfully.

"Yes, he has a considerable fortune now; but I have no doubt that he will squander it away," said Lady Leveson. "But, whatever folly he may commit, it is the most unlikely thing in the world that he should fall in love with Miss Clevedon. They know each other much

too well for that, depend upon it, Amy.
So don't be discouraged, dear; and, above
all things, don't try to compete with her
in her own line. Let her talk politics
and philosophy as much as she likes;
it will only the better set off your un-
assuming, feminine qualities, which young
Jocelyn will appreciate, sooner or later,
you may be sure."

"If there is one thing I specially
hate," said Amy, angrily, "it is to hear
women, and particularly girls like Silvia
Clevedon, talking politics."

"It is, of course, very bold and un-
feminine," said Lady Leveson, decisively;
"but some women do not care for that.
And I imagine Miss Clevedon is utterly
regardless of any construction that may
be put upon her actions or opinions.

You know, her mother said she was quite a Radical."

"But what is a Radical, mamma?" asked Amy. "I am sure, if any one asked me, I couldn't exactly tell."

"I should be puzzled myself to define the exact meaning of the term," said Lady Leveson; "but, as generally accepted, it means something very rough, and low, and coarse-mannered, and badly dressed. I never before heard of or met a young lady of good blood and family who dared own to being a Radical. Disappointed younger sons sometimes go in for that sort of thing, and, of course, their relations and friends drop them, and no people of our set would look at them. Miss Clevedon seems to have things pretty much her own way here, however."

"Just imagine the absurdity of her walking down the garden, talking to her maid, this morning!" said Amy. "I believe she did it on purpose, because she knew we should be waiting for her and should see her, and she felt that she would appear to advantage."

"Amy! Amy!" said her mother, "you must not be spiteful. "Such a speech as that would set Gilbert Jocelyn against you instantly. Go to bed, child, and see what a sound night's rest will do towards reconciling you to the place. I will promise you not to stop here too long, if that will please you."

With a kiss, Lady Leveson sent her daughter to her room, and, after a few moments' meditation, rang for her maid, who undertook the disrobing and preparation of her ladyship for the night.

In the mean time, in another part of the house, a mother and daughter were together, talking. Silvia had only been in her room a minute or two, and was listening to the chatter of the pretty maid with whom she had walked down the garden that morning, when Mrs. Clevedon entered, and, dismissing the maid with a hasty "You can go, Ellen," took a seat on the broad lounge, one end of which Silvia occupied.

"Why, mother dear, this is out of all precedent!" said Silvia, smiling brightly. "Now, don't spoil the surprise by saying you have come to scold me."

"Yes, I have, indeed, Silvia," said her mother, seriously, "and you must listen to me."

"I will listen," answered Silvia; "but

what can it be about? I thought I had behaved splendidly to-day. I asked Miss Leveson to go out with me this morning, and she wouldn't. I sat with her and her mother for full an hour on the lawn this afternoon, talking about mutual acquaintances, and discovering that I strongly disliked all the people they strongly liked; and I encouraged Gilbert to flirt with the girl all the evening. Come, mother, what more could I do?"

"My dear child," said Mrs. Clevedon, taking no notice of the humorous twinkle in her daughter's fine eyes, "your father is very vexed indeed at your expressing your opinions so freely as you did to-night before Lady Leveson and her daughter and Gilbert Jocelyn. It's bad enough for you to have the opinions, he says, but it's positively wilful of you to display them."

" Why, mother, mother !" cried Silvia, "what are you teaching me? Surely, you would not have me dissimulate my opinions, whatever they may be."

" Of course not," said Mrs. Clevedon ; "but you might just as well hold your tongue."

"But that is dissimulation, mother," expostulated Silvia. "That is leading people to think I have no opinions at all, which is a direct untruth."

" I know that well enough," said Mrs. Clevedon, impatiently. " But your father does not think women's opinions of importance, one way or another ; therefore it would be no great fault in you to keep them to yourself."

"On the other hand," said Silvia, smiling, "if women's opinions are so unimportant, it surely does not matter of what shade they are. Either women are reasonable beings, or they are dolls. If they are reasonable beings, they have a right to their free and independent opinions; if they are dolls, their opinions are of no consequence. Father inclines to think of us as dolls, I know, and therefore he ought to let me say whatever I like, express any special fancy that strikes me, since I am only a woman."

"But, my dear child," said Mrs. Clevedon, "you know, it is so very singular for a young lady like yourself to have political views, and such political views, too!"

Here Silvia laughed. " Ah! mother, dear," she cried, "now you have touched the kernel of father's complaint. It isn't so much that he objects to my having some interest in politics, as that he dislikes the particular party in politics with which I most sympathize."

" However that may be, Silvia," said her mother—" and you had better talk it over with your father than with me, for I frankly confess that I know very little on the subject, beyond that all my family were Tories, and I was born a Tory, and a Tory I intend to remain to the end of my days—at all events, your father told me to tell you distinctly that he did not like to hear such views as yours expressed, and that he hoped you would keep them in the background

—at least, while we have guests in the house."

"What a dear illiberal old father he is!" said Silvia, with another laugh. "Tories were always tyrants, you see, mother, and tyrants they will remain. Father wants to gag me, just as people were gagged by the Tories of the Middle Ages. But he need not have minded my expatiating on Radical principles in Lady Leveson's presence. I am certain she does not know Radical from Tory opinions, unless the difference be pointed out to her. She has perhaps a dim idea that a Radical is the worse of the two, because he has generally been the poorer."

"I don't think your father is so particular about Lady Leveson as about

Gilbert," said Mrs. Clevedon. "He wants Gilbert to think well of you, and was very vexed at your walking about the grounds this morning with your maid—with Ellen."

"Oh, mother," cried Silvia, her face growing suddenly grave, "why should I not walk down the garden with Ellen? If you knew, too, what I was saying to her, you could not blame me. I believe that the few words I said to her have kept her free from wrong—for the time, at least."

"Neither your father nor I doubt your heart or your principle, dear child," said Mrs. Clevedon, leaning forward to kiss her daughter's forehead. "But all people don't know you so well as we do. Gilbert may think it strange."

"As for Gilbert," said Silvia, "he knows all my enormities of opinion already. I told him that I had a leaning towards Radical views, when we were out this morning, yet he did not refuse to walk home with me."

"By-the-by," said Mrs. Clevedon, gently, "that reminds me, also, that I wished to tell you not to be too familiar with Gilbert, or go out with him alone again in the same way, because Lady Leveson made remarks."

"Lady Leveson may make whole volumes of remarks," said Silvia, quietly, "and I shall not give in to them. Neither father nor you have ever objected to my friendship with Gilbert, and Lady Leveson's opinion is perfectly immaterial to me. I cannot think why you asked them here, mother. They are unsympathetic to us all."

"I hardly know, beyond that I had found them very friendly in town," said Mrs. Clevedon, "and they seemed most anxious to be asked. I shall leave you now, Silvia dear. Just think over your father's wishes, and try to fall in with them better."

And with an affectionate "Good night," the mother and daughter separated.

Silvia sat alone for some time, meditating on her mother's remarks. The suggestion that she should disguise her thoughts and feelings because of Gilbert Jocelyn, had been most unwelcome to her. She was naturally frankness itself, and it galled her to hear that she was

expected to maintain a false appearance
in his eyes, and that she was believed
capable of it. She could not understand
her father's repugnance to her open expression of opinion, and still less could
she understand his abhorrence of all that
was most sympathetic to her. How was
it, she asked herself, that while he was
full of thought and consideration for
Lady Leveson, whom he did not really
like, he would have died sooner than
have made one courteous, condescending
remark to a servant who had been in
his house more than twenty years?
How was it that, while he recognized
the patrician prettiness of Amy Leveson,
he would not see the rustic comeliness of
Ellen, the maid? How was it, in short,
that his heart was glowing with warmth

for one small section of the human race, and cold as marble to others ?

The reverie was broken in upon by the entrance of the maid, who had been sent in, she said, by Mrs. Clevedon.

"But I don't want you, Ellen," said Silvia, smiling kindly at the girl. "You can go to bed; I am sure you want rest. You must promise me, however, not to spend another night as you did the last. You must try to forget it all, and take no notice of the temptations thrust upon you. You are sure of yourself, are you not ?" Silvia added, placing her hand confidentially on the girl's arm, and looking at her seriously, even solemnly.

"I hope so," the maid replied, her face flushing painfully. "I should be ashamed of going wrong, if it's only because of your kindness. If all poor girls like me could find some one so good as you, miss, to help them, we shouldn't so often go wrong."

"That's true enough, I am sure," said Silvia, reflectively. "As a rule, I know that no one helps you to keep right, and every one blames you when you 'go wrong.' Still, this is nothing more serious than a few light words. You will find that your friend is merely trying to pass the time that hangs heavily on his hands, by a little random flattery."

The girl made no answer, but with a subdued "Good night," left the room.

And Silvia was free to let her thoughts run wild.

CHAPTER III.

Two days later, Gilbert Jocelyn announced, at lunch-time, that a cricket-match was going forward below the Bench, at the other end of the town; that a number of ladies had assembled to watch the contest, and that Miss Leveson and Miss Clevedon must put in an appearance also.

"My dear Gilbert, if you are going to run after all the cricket-matches that take place in this neighbourhood, you will never have a moment's respite," said Silvia. "The whole population is cricket-mad; and even the curate takes upon himself the ignoble duties of scout, occasionally."

"Do you play, Mr. Jocelyn?" asked Amy Leveson.

"No. I really never could get up sufficient enthusiasm on the subject," said Jocelyn; "and I was wondering just now, when I saw all the fellows exerting themselves so unconscionably for the sake of hitting a ball, what could be the incentive to the sport."

"They had better play cricket, however, than do nothing at all," said Silvia; "and as they are too gentlemanly to do manual labour, and too foolish for intellectual labour, I suppose sport is the only thing left for them as a means of passing the time."

" They are men of independent fortune, Silvia," said the admiral, " and are not required to work.—All the families living in this district," he added, turning to Lady Leveson, " are rich and well connected, and almost all the cricketers of whom Sylvia speaks, are men whose positions are ready made for them."

" Still, an active brain cannot remain idle, father," said Silvia, " and you must allow that the young men of good family who pervade the neighbourhood are singularly dull and uninteresting."

" By the way," said Jocelyn, " I met a man on the cricket-ground whom I knew rather intimately at one time, at Oxford. His name is Philip Royle. I asked him how he got down here, and he tells me that he is staying with a friend who has a pretty little property in this neighbourhood."

"Do you know any particular good point in him?" asked Silvia, whose face had flushed at the mention of the name, and whose eyes were almost flashing.

Jocelyn laughed.

"Well, he was considered rather wild and dissipated, and difficult to deal with," he answered. "I don't know much beyond that. He is a clever fellow, and ambitious, in his way. He was wonderfully amusing too, and always knew everything about everybody. There were a number of ladies about him to-day, laughing immoderately at his lightest word. To return to the question of the match, however. You will come, won't you, just to glance at the fun?"

" I should like it of all things in the world," said Amy Leveson, to whom the opportunity for flirtation was a new hope ; and her decided expression of opinion necessarily led to a deliberate plan, the result of which was that, early in the afternoon, Mrs. Clevedon and the two girls (Lady Leveson had begged them to leave her in her low chair on the lawn with a novel), escorted by Gilbert Jocelyn, appeared on the broad plain beyond the Bench.

" You don't want to go and join all those people under the awning over there, do you?" said Jocelyn, pointing to groups of ladies who were seated at some distance in rows, and evidently going into the game *con amore.*

Amy Leveson, in her character of gentle woman, did not like to oppose Jocelyn's evident preference, and Silvia said with perfect truth that she, for her part, would rather stay where she was. Jocelyn therefore fetched a couple of chairs for Mrs. Clevedon and Miss Leveson, and Silvia sat down on the grass, and gazed thoughtfully at the wide expanse of undulating ground in the distance, varied by the nearer plain, on which the cricketers were disporting themselves—the whole scene presided over by the stiff hill, on the summit of which was the bench that gave its name to the spot.

Silvia was roused in a few moments from her reverie by hearing Jocelyn exclaim, " Royle has found us out, and

is coming across to us. Do you see
him, Silvia ? ''

" Yes, I see him," answered Silvia.

" Don't you think he's very handsome,
Miss Clevedon ? '' said Amy Leveson,
watching the approaching figure.

" I suppose he is," said Silvia; " every
one says so ; but, for my part, I am
quite blind to his beauty, because of my
dislike for the man's character."

At this juncture, Royle reached the
party, and having been introduced to
Miss Leveson, opened a fire of small-
talk, thereby making himself vastly
agreeable to that young lady. He
glanced every now and then at Silvia,
who had only vouchsafed him a most
formal bow, as if he wished her to join
in the conversation. But she was per-

fectly silent, and did not appear to hear what was going on. When they had talked of a thousand and one nothings, of the gayest balls of the season, the most rollicking garden-parties, the most amenable chaperones, the best theatres, and had exhausted their remarks on the rusticity of the pretty forest village hard by, Royle turned towards Silvia, and said—

"Miss Clevedon, you have not spoken at all. I have had all the talk to myself."

"It would have been cruel in me to deprive you of the privilege," said Silvia. "I hope you have enjoyed it."

"You don't approve of Royle's trivial gossip, do you, Silvia?" said Jocelyn, good-humouredly.

"I can't say that I don't approve of it," said Silvia, quite unconcernedly, "for I have not heard one single word that Mr. Royle has said.—However," she added, turning with a smile to Royle, "if you will begin again, I will try to listen, and will tell you, when you have finished, whether or no I approve."

"You are in for it, Royle," laughed Jocelyn. "Miss Clevedon is opening her batteries. In the mean time, I shall take Miss Leveson to glance at the cricketers' more practical sport, if she will come."

Miss Leveson was only too delighted, and Royle was left to argue with Silvia, under Mrs. Clevedon's sagacious eye. He was a bold man in every sense, and he put his thoughts into unmistakably plain speech, utterly undaunted by the presence of a third person.

"Miss Clevedon," he began, "I am sure that you are angry with me for some cause or another. There is something in your mind about me that you do not like to express, perhaps; I have forfeited your good opinion, I am afraid."

"You would appear to be a keen observer," said Silvia.

The young man's face flushed, and he exclaimed, "Then it's true that I have offended you!"

"You have not offended me personally," said Silvia, calmly. "You have simply set at nought all my ideas of the honour and chivalry towards weakness and trustfulness that should characterize a true gentleman in the highest sense of the word—that is all."

"Silvia! Silvia!" said her mother. "What are you saying? What do you mean?"

"Mr. Royle pressed me to tell him what I thought, mother," said Silvia, "and I have told him the truth. He knows what I mean, I have no doubt."

Royle had drawn himself up stiffly, and now asked, with some show of resentment, if Miss Clevedon wished to insult him.

"I had no wish one way or the other," replied Silvia; "I merely answered your question. In that wretched state of society in which we all move, many persons who meet apparently on the best of terms, day after day, are not more flatteringly disposed towards each other than I am towards you. So we need not get up a quarrel, unless you think it necessary to the preservation of your dignity."

"But won't you tell me what I have done specially to vex you?" urged Royle.

Silvia, for the first time during the colloquy, raised her eyes to his face, and met his earnest, anxious look. "I cannot tell you," she said at last, "but your own conscience can."

Royle turned quickly away, and walked back towards the cricketing centre with sharp, impatient steps. "I see what she means," he muttered to himself. "That silly little maid of hers has told her of my absurd folly in chattering to her. Still, it's preposterous that she should talk to me in that style, about chivalry and honour, as if one couldn't laugh with a lady's-maid with impunity! Perhaps the empty-headed little vixen has taken my nonsense to be sober truth, and has confided all her woes to Miss Clevedon's willing ears. Women never can hold their tongues, I know. However, that young person from Clevedon House has seen the last of my smiles, I can assure her. As for Miss Clevedon, she has evidently taken a strong dislike to me; I can't find favour there. What an unfortunate fellow I am!"

It was with a certain sense of defeat and dissatisfaction that he rejoined the party of ladies he had left a few moments before, in order to speak to the Clevedons. He was assailed by a formidable spinster immediately, and asked " what he thought of Miss Clevedon." But he evaded the question, and the combined curiosity of all the womanhood around him did not succeed in drawing forth any opinion as to Miss Clevedon's personal or mental qualities.

In the mean time, Mrs. Clevedon had remonstrated with Silvia on her forcible mode of explaining herself. "You know, my dear," she said, "every one is not used to your strange frankness; and I am afraid, if you tell people what you really think, as you did just now to that young man, you will make yourself crowds of enemies."

"But Mr. Royle deserved to be snubbed," said Silvia.

"What has he done? What do you

know about him?" asked Mrs. Clevedon.

"Why, mother," said Silvia, in a low
voice, "Ellen has told me that she has
met him several times in the lanes, when
she has been going backwards and forwards into the village, and he has paid
her compliments and talked to her, and
has, in fact, quite turned her head."

"You say Ellen," exclaimed Mrs.
Clevedon—"whom do you mean? You
are surely not alluding to your maid
Ellen?"

"Yes, I am, mother," said Silvia.
"Why not?"

"Why, it's positively ridiculous of you
to talk to a man about the honour and
chivalry of a true gentleman, when he
has only been gossiping with your maid,"

said Mrs. Clevedon, angrily. "I thought you had heard of some serious wrong-doing of his, or I should never have allowed you to attack him in that manner."

"But, mother, I don't see why Ellen's feelings are not to be consulted in the matter," expostulated Silvia. "He has flattered her; he has made her discontented with her servant's life; he has given her all sorts of ideas that she need never have had, and she seems inclined to fall into an idolatrous love of him, because he is a gentleman, and has told her that she is pretty. I think a true gentleman should be most careful not to endanger the peace of mind of honest girls, who are earning their living by something very like drudgery. If Mr.

Royle should flirt too boldly with Miss
Leveson, why, to begin with, she is used
to flirtation, and will know how to defend
herself, and all society will be up in arms
to protect her interests. If Mr. Royle
trifle with her affections, every one will
be ready to punish him for the enormity.
But he may trifle with Ellen's affections
as much as he please; he may break her
heart, in fact, and no one thinks the
worse of him for it. That is what I think
so unjust, mother."

"Oh, nonsense, Silvia! I am quite
tired of your wild ideas," said Mrs.
Clevedon. "To begin with, I have no
doubt that Ellen has grossly exaggerated
anything that Mr. Royle has said to her.
There is no limit to the vanity of her
class of people, and she has taken literally

and seriously that which he meant as a joke. At all events, it is not for you to talk to a young man about his flirtations with a lady's-maid, and I shall take care to show Mr. Royle that I did not approve of your ridiculous, high-flown language. I never heard of anything so absurd. How he must be laughing at you!"

"He didn't seem inclined to laugh," answered Silvia; "on the contrary, he looked grave, almost stern."

"Well, Silvia, you've despatched Royle, I see," broke in Jocelyn's voice at this juncture, as he brought Miss Leveson back to Mrs. Clevedon's side.

"Indeed she has," said Mrs. Clevedon. "She has almost told him he was not a gentleman, or a man of honour or of truth, because he has been joking and laughing with one of the maids."

"Whew!" muttered Jocelyn, with an unmistakable expression of disapproval on his face. "Did you go into that question with him, Silvia?"

"Not quite as boldly as you might infer," said Silvia, in a low voice. "But pray let the subject drop. I am sorry I have vexed you, mother."

So saying, she turned away, and, with the observation that she wanted to climb the hill and see how the plain looked from the Bench, began a leisurely ascent. When she rejoined her party, Royle was apparently forgotten.

On the evening of that same day, however, when the dinner at Clevedon House was over, and the coffee, served on the lawn, was being lazily partaken of by the diners, Lady Leveson said suddenly, "Who is this Mr. Royle of whom my daughter has spoken to me, Mrs. Clevedon?"

"I really know nothing of him," that lady answered, "beyond that we have met him often lately, at the houses of very good people."

"You don't know of what family he is, then?" said Lady Leveson.

"No. I have, moreover, never heard his family mentioned," replied Mrs. Clevedon. "He was introduced to us at first as a chum of one of the sons of the house where we met, and since then he has spoken to us whenever we have seen him, and I have never troubled myself about his connections."

"It strikes me," said Jocelyn, good-humouredly, "that his connections are not his strong point."

"Oh, indeed," said Lady Leveson, fully prepared to drop all interest in the young man. "You knew him at Oxford, did you not, Mr. Jocelyn?"

"Yes, I saw a great deal of him there," said Jocelyn. "He was an odd fellow, and at one time we threatened to become fast friends, but gradually he took to reading hard——"

"And you took to boating hard, I presume?" said Silvia, laughing.

"Exactly—the very thing I was going to say," replied Jocelyn, nodding to Silvia, with a smile; then continuing, "and I saw less of him. The men who knew him best said he was dissipated and wild; but they said that, at the same time, he worked steadily, and seemed terribly anxious to get on. Young North, a friend of mine, who knew him better than I, used to vow that the fellow was a thorough *roturier*, you know, who had wriggled into the university by hook or by crook. He was never heard to make any allusion to his family, or to any friends apart from those he had made at Oxford, and North had a rooted idea that Royle's people were in trade, and lived somewhere in Camden Town, or some place of the kind, because he said Royle had so many packages and hampers and letters from a London suburb of the rank of Camden Town — I think he mentioned that objectionable locality itself."

"North is a man I should like to know," said Silvia, with a smile.

"North, you see," said Jocelyn, apologetically, "is of a first-rate family, and is very aristocratic and exclusive in his ideas, and it worried him to think that he might have chosen a genuine pleb. for his friend. Finally, when he had found out a score of little things tending to cast a shade on Royle's parentage, he contrived to drop him, bit by bit. He really liked him, I believe, but he couldn't put up with the continual questions and suggestions as to Royle's family."

"A noble friend!" remarked Silvia.

"What a pity!" ejaculated Lady Leveson. "And yet, Amy told me he was quite handsome and agreeable, and talked about society, and the London season, and so on."

"He can be excessively agreeable, when he chooses," said Jocelyn, "and he goes into very good society in town. You see, he is a bachelor, and he is effective personally; then he dances well, and is very clever at amateur theatricals, and that kind of thing; and as long as he confines himself to cultivating the friendship of the sons of a family, he is very welcome. But he will find it remarkably difficult to marry in the circles he frequents."

"Has he no mother or father, then?" asked Silvia.

"No sign of a family has been seen by any of his friends," said Jocelyn. "You can't ask a fellow point-blank whether he has any family—it would be insulting, you know; and as he doesn't volunteer any information, nothing is known. He's a clever fellow, however, and is sure to make his way, sooner or later."

And here the conversation turned to other subjects.

That night, when Silvia was in her room, Ellen the maid knocked at the door, and entering, in obedience to Silvia's injunction, stepped gently up to her young mistress, who was sitting by the open window.

"What's the matter now, Ellen?" asked Silvia.

"I wished to tell you, miss," said Ellen, looking down, and fingering her apron nervously as she spoke, "that I met that gentleman, Mr. Royle, again this evening, and—and—— "

" Is it too dreadful to be told ? " suggested Silvia, with a smile.

"Oh no," replied Ellen, looking up for a moment to smile brightly in return. "He told me that he was very sorry if he'd disturbed me or vexed me in any way, that he was sure I was a good girl, and he hoped I'd keep so, and he said he was very much ashamed of having joked me or teased me. So that's all over, miss."

" I am very glad of it," answered Silvia. "You see now how little Mr. Royle's pretty speeches and compliments were worth. A man in his position has to pass his life paying compliments, in order to secure standing-ground. You must try to forget it all, Ellen, and make yourself happy here."

"I shall always be happy enough as long as you are here," murmured the girl.

When Ellen had been sent away, Silvia had a few moments' reflection on the incidents of the day, and she could not but congratulate herself that she had done at least a little good. "At all events," she murmured to herself, thinking of Philip Royle, as she gazed at the broad expanse of lawn, field, and forest, upon which the placid moon was shining—"at all events, he is not a coward."

CHAPTER IV.

As Jocelyn was strolling through the village a week later, and was glancing towards the big bow-window of the Eagle coffee-room, a tall figure advanced from the terrace that ran along the front of the house, and Philip Royle—for it was he—waylaid Jocelyn, and begged him to stop and talk with him. Therefore Jocelyn turned aside from the walk he had planned, to lounge in the cool shade of the creepers and roses that covered the whole frontage of the Eagle Inn.

The village consisted of one street, and that street was built on a steep hill, so that when you stood at the summit of it, with the Eagle Inn to your left, and the fine Gothic church to your right, you could look down to where the last few straggling houses stood in the valley, and presently, beyond the valley, rose another hill, crowned by the bench of which we have already heard. The Eagle, on the crest of the high ground, and the Foresters', at the end of the village in the plain, represented the social as well as the actual extremes of Lyndwood. The Eagle was patronised by the aristocrats who came into the neighbourhood; the great cricketers' banquets were held in the Eagle dining-room; it was at the

Eagle that the people who drove over to Lyndwood for the day, put up; and at the Eagle only could the London papers be seen. The Foresters' Inn was of an entirely different character. It was clean and comfortable as the great Eagle itself, but its few frequenters were of an entirely different class to those of the rival hostelry. The vehicles to be seen outside the Foresters' were mostly farmers' dog-carts, hired traps of various ignominious forms, and rough-and-ready donkey carts. None of the villagers concerned themselves at all as to the success of the Foresters'; but the Eagle was the apple of Lyndwood's eye.

When there was a fresh arrival, when a new relay of trunks was deposited in the familiar doorway, over which

the imperial bird was ever spreading
its wings, the excitement in the long
street was considerable. The butcher
hard by peered curiously over his broad
counter, and forgot to answer his cus-
tomers' questions in his intense interest
in the Eagle's prosperity; the saddler's
pretty daughter ran to her father's shop
door in order to grant the new-comer
a vision of her plump and rosy beauty;
the two pale and faded sisters who represented the millinery force of Lyndwood, came timidly from their sanctum
of cap-blocks and bonnet-shapes, to
peep at the ladies' head-gear; while the
owners of the little cake and sweet-
stuff shop near the Foresters' gazed
longingly up the hill at the stir and
bustle in front of the Eagle. Presently,

the " trap " would be turned into the
stables round the corner; the grooms
and ostlers would disappear, on drinking
thoughts intent; the gay parties would
flutter from the terrace and the doorway
to the long, lofty rooms of the old inn;
and the butcher down the street would
turn his dreamy eyes back to his business; the saddler's pretty daughter, with
a half-drawn sigh that no gallant eye
had lit upon her rustic comeliness, would
re-enter upon the routine of her daily
household duties; the faded milliners
would resume their work with an un-
attainable ideal of lightness and bright-
ness and grace in their mind's eye; and
the hard-featured keeper of the cakes
and sweetmeats would cry to her bed-
ridden mother in the room behind the

shop, as she doled out a pennyworth of "brandy balls" to a chubby eight-year old customer—

"There's a fresh party of gentry arrived up the hill, mother. Did you ever know anything like that there Eagle!"

The "gentry" certainly knew how to choose, for the Eagle was as picturesque a place as could well have been found throughout the county. The house seemed buried in rich foliage and flower. The roses nodded in at the windows, and the creeper clung lovingly about the trellised porch, while the terrace, rising at one end considerably above the level of the street, was carpeted and shaded with green growth and ornamented with the splendour of the roses.

The young men who had seated themselves in front of one of the long French
windows that opened on to the terrace,
smoked their cigars in silence for a few
minutes, Jocelyn's fair, smooth face and
quiet eyes forming a perfect contrast to
the southern type of Royle's head.

"This is by no means a bad place,"
said Jocelyn at length. "I hate the
country, as a rule; but I must confess
that Lyndwood has a special charm of
its own."

"Has it?" said Royle. "Why, where
does the special charm live?"

Jocelyn laughed. "As if I should
tell you, if I knew," he replied.

"You are stopping with the Clevedons, are you not?" said Royle, somewhat irrelevantly.

"I hardly call it stopping with them," said Jocelyn. "Clevedon House is like my home, and a very pleasant home, too, I can assure you."

"I don't doubt it," replied Royle, shortly; adding, "you have a large party there, have you not?"

"No," said Jocelyn; "we are quite alone. The Levesons have been on a visit, but they have gone off, thoroughly disgusted, I fancy, with the flavour of Miss Clevedon's conversation; and, to tell you the truth, I don't think any one regrets them. The girl was pretty."

"But terribly foolish, I should think," remarked Royle.

"Of course she was," assented Jocelyn; "but I don't mind foolish girls, I must own. Now, Amy Leveson could in her

own way give you an answer, and knew
how to hold her ground, in that sort
of light fencing that we call flirtation;
but, of course, if you put her to discuss
with Miss Clevedon, why, she would be
smashed to atoms in a moment. Then,
Miss Clevedon is a genius, and can
silence most of us, if she choose."

Royle laughed, saying, "She has certainly got a tongue of her own."

"By-the-by, you have had a specimen
of her attacks, have you not?" asked
Jocelyn.

Royle bent his head gravely, and
answered, "Yes; she was good enough
to let me know how bad an opinion she
had of me, and I was the more sorry
for it, from the fact that she compelled
my admiration and respect. You should

have seen her, Jocelyn, while she was speaking to me; she looked superb, and I really felt ashamed of the trivialities of which she accused me."

Jocelyn laughed gaily. "I see she hit you hard, Royle."

"She made an impression upon my mind, I confess," said Royle, "and I have thought again and again that I should like to extenuate myself somewhat in her eyes."

"My dear fellow," said Jocelyn, "there is no need of extenuation and all that sort of thing, I am certain. She has forgotten the grievance against you and yourself, depend upon it, by this time. She speaks energetically, but she doesn't mean or wish to hurt any one's feelings. I've had a lecture this morning on my idleness, but I don't mind it; in fact, it rather amuses me."

"I should like to hear her ideas on idleness," said Royle.

"They are very soon told," said Jocelyn, stretching himself out indolently. "She thinks every man ought to work for his living, and that those men who are born rich enough to be independent of work, should work notwithstanding, and devote their money to the amelioration of less fortunate lives."

"I wonder what she would say to a man who not only does not work, but lives on the work of others whom he is not honest enough to own?" muttered Royle, bitterly.

Jocelyn looked keenly at him, and

then answered, lightly, "I only hope there will be a third person on the spot when she meets such a man, or the result might really be homicidal."

Royle did not answer; and, after a few moments, Jocelyn rose leisurely to his feet, and protested that he must be off. "I promised Miss Clevedon most faithfully," he observed, "that if I did not work, I would at least walk, and I am afraid that she would be very hard upon me if she found my walk had not extended beyond the Eagle. When do you go up to town, Royle?"

"In a few days, or a week," replied Royle. "I've left my friends, and am stopping here."

"Then I shall see you before you go," said Jocelyn; and he added, as he smiled and shook hands with Royle, "I am in a hurry to get off, as I am in some trepidation lest Miss Clevedon should come along on that spirited animal of hers, and should attack me before the whole town!"

Royle's discomfiture was complete. He had felt certain that Jocelyn would ask him to call at Clevedon House; he had even hoped that he might be invited to lunch that day; but it was evident that Jocelyn knew he would not be welcome. Miss Clevedon had decided opinions; she disliked him, and there was nothing to be done, he said to himself, but to go back to town, and not to trouble himself any more as to what she thought. He lingered on at the Eagle, however, day after day, with a vague sense of hope

and expectancy, but at length resolved
to break the absurd spell growing round
him.

Accordingly, he paid all the visits
in the neighbourhood that he was bound
to pay before leaving, one early August
afternoon, and in the evening he sent
his luggage up to the station, some five
miles from the Eagle. He should leave
by the first train in the morning, he
said, and did not want any conveyance—
he should walk to the station. Mine
host of the Eagle protested that a trap
should be ready for him at any hour he
liked to mention; but Royle was bent
on a long walk in the morning air. It
would do him good, he said to himself—
it would drive his wild ideas away. And
so it fell out that Royle started alone

on his early walk through the "happy autumn fields" towards the station.

The way lay by hill and dale, by streams and fields and wide pine plantations, and Royle looked round him regretfully at the beauty of the scene. Everything was serene and quiet; not a human being was to be seen on all the wide expanse of ground, and the only disturbers of the stillness of the air were the birds, as they hopped joyously from twig to twig, from branch to branch, of the noble trees that lined the road. The morning sunshine lit the scene with its brightest beams, and all looked so clear and serene and sylvan, that Royle could hardly believe that in a few short hours he would have reached the dull, black, smoky metropolis—London.

He turned aside from the main road presently, and followed a faintly indicated foot-track that would lead him to the station through the greenest and gayest of glades, the most picturesque bits of fringe of the forest.

He walked slowly enough in this deep seclusion, his eyes bent on the ground, his thoughts taking the strangest forms and fancies. Suddenly, an instinct made him raise his head, and he saw, only a few yards in front of him, a lady and a horse. The lady had dismounted and was walking leisurely along, holding up her habit with one hand, and with the other now and then plucking a stray fern leaf, now and then stroking the docile horse's neck. Royle looked earnestly, and his heart gave a great throb.

Surely he could not be mistaken? That
tall slender figure, those masses of bright
brown hair, that finely set head, could
only belong to one person; and even as
he wondered, a turn of the head showed
him the face he wished to see, and he
sprang forward eagerly and quickly, exclaiming—

"I am so glad to meet you, Miss
Clevedon."

Silvia, for it was she, was evidently
startled at the rencontre; and while he
told her that he was on his way to the
station, she stood still, holding her horse
by the bridle, thereby giving Royle to
understand that she wished him to leave
her to her ramble. But he was not to
be deterred when he had a definite idea
in his mind, and seeing that which she

intended to convey to him, he said—
" Will you not let me walk beside you
a little way, Miss Clevedon ? I should
very much like to speak a few words to
you, if I may."

" I cannot refuse to listen," said Silvia,
walking on slowly then, " but you must
say what you wish to say quickly."

He was silent for a few moments, as
they advanced side by side through the
tangle of fern and weed and moss ; he
glanced at Silvia's handsome face once
or twice, as if he were lingering on its
features and expression, and at last he
began—

" Miss Clevedon, I know how badly
you think of me, and I know that there
may be a little ground for your dislike,
but I should like to explain to you, if

I may, that I was not nearly so bad as I seemed."

"I am glad to hear it," answered Silvia, "and I am sorry that you should think yourself bound to explain. My opinion is of no real consequence to you, and I had no intention of persecuting you with my dislike."

"But I wanted you to think well of me," pleaded Royle, earnestly.

"What an extraordinary person you are!" said Silvia, smiling. "I cannot understand why you should be so anxious in the matter. Still, since you so particularly wish to know what I think, I may tell you that I have heard how you terminated the affair of which I disapproved. I acquit you of anything worse than lightness and thoughtlessness, and I only wish I were powerful enough to influence you in the future. And now I must turn back. You will lose your train, too, I am afraid."

"No, I have plenty of time," he answered; then, as Silvia stood still, evidently wishing him to leave her, he said, hastily, "I will go; don't be afraid. You needn't grudge me another moment. I should like not only to have explained to you my apparent misbehaviour, which was nothing more than lightness and thoughtlessness, as you say, but to have asked you to tell me some of your thoughts on man's work, as you told them to Jocelyn."

"You forget that Mr. Jocelyn is like a brother to me, and that you are all but a stranger," said Silvia, gravely.

"I forgot—yes, it's true," muttered Royle. "I have spoken too frankly. Never mind what I have said; try to forget it all."

Silvia had gathered up her skirts while he was speaking, and in answer to his low "Good-bye, Miss Clevedon," bowed to him, and was turning away. But he sprang forward, saying—

"Won't you shake hands with me?"

Silvia put her hand in his, frankly, murmuring "Good-bye" in astonishment; and he pressed it so tightly for a moment that he positively hurt her.

Then, he lifted his hat and strode away. He never turned to look back. She saw his tall, stalwart figure disappear among the trees, and before long she heard the railway whistle, and knew that he must have reached the station—that he must have gone.

"I met Mr. Royle this morning, Gilbert," said Silvia, at breakfast, an hour later. "He was on his road to the station."

"Off to London, was he?" said Jocelyn. "He has seemed strangely unsettled in his mind lately, and I'm glad he has decided to leave."

Silvia thought also that he was strangely unsettled in his mind, but she said nothing.

CHAPTER V.

LAUREL LODGE was as pretty a house as could be found among the many pretty houses in St. John's Wood. It stood in a small garden, and in front there were two fine elm trees, that shaded it from the keen gaze of observers on the other side of the road; while the strip of lawn, at the back of the house, was dotted with sturdy laurel bushes. A luxuriant jessamine twined about the balcony of the back drawing-room, and the slender iron steps leading from the window to the lawn were almost hid in the fragrant growth. The house looked like a toy building, rather than a human habitation —it was so neat and white and trim, with its pretty portico, its huge bow windows, its graceful *entourage* of flower-garden, lawn, and shrub, its slanting-roofed balconies, its covering of sweet-scented jessamine; and it was hard to believe that the prosaic conditions of life were being worked out day by day within the four white walls.

Small as the house appeared, it contained a number of rooms, and sheltered a number of human beings, as a glance into the general sitting-room and dining-room will show. The windows were wide open, for the evening air was hot and heavy, and the gentle swaying of the elm branches in the mild August breeze was refreshing to the cheerful party congregated about the massive family table.

The group was a comely one—an unmistakably English home picture. The head of the household lay back in a capacious armchair, with the morning's *Times* in his hands and shielding his face, and the daughters, each busy at some harmless occupation, chatted and laughed together happily. There were five sisters, and one of them, who seemed older and graver than the others, evidently filled the mother's place. It was she who glanced periodically at her father, to see if he were disturbed by the gay voices; it was to her that the servant turned for directions when she was summoned; it was to her that the girls appealed in support of this or in deprecation of that; and before her stood a basket piled with unmistakable household sewing, while her sisters were busy with the various, somewhat unpracticable forms of fancy work.

The sisters differed considerably in person, as in character. Hester, the eldest, who had taken her dead mother's place in the home, was as grave and dignified as Ellen, who came next, was lively and brilliant, and, if truth must be told, somewhat vulgar. The third, Julia, was engaged to be married, and, on the strength of her proud position among the sisters, gave herself little matronly airs, and professed a sagacity and prudence strangely at variance with her twenty-three years. The fourth,

Charlotte, was an enthusiastic upholder of the High Church party, as represented in her district by a good-looking, pale-faced curate, who wore a broad black sash round his waist and buckles to his shoes; and her devotion took the form of decking her person with cross and crucifix, and medals and various symbols, so that she rattled like a bunch of keys when she walked. And the fifth and youngest of the family, Effie, who was between eighteen and nineteen, was so gentle and loving and clinging in her nature, that she seemed hardly to have any decided tastes of her own, from her large sympathies with every living crea-ture, and her utter forgetfulness of self. A sweet face it was that Effie bent over her embroidery—a face above the hoy-

denish beauty of her three elder sisters,
and quite apart from the staid gravity
that characterized the eldest, Hester.
There was something spiritual in the
gaze of her large dark eyes. It seemed
as if the soul of the dying mother, who
had breathed her last when Effie was
born, had given them their strange,
wistful pathos and earnestness; and
Effie's father, ordinary, prosaic, com-
mercial man as he was, often caught
a glance from their blue depths that
brought a vivid remembrance of his early
love to his mind.

The girls were talking with considerable animation on this particular evening.
They had been to a croquet gathering
during the afternoon at a neighbour's, and
were discussing the incidents with zest.

"Did you ever see anything like the affectation of Minnie Maldon, though, Julia?" said Ellen, vivaciously. "She told Mr. Wentworth at first, seeing that he was a clergyman, that she never played croquet, for it was so trivial and uninteresting; but when she found that he wasn't too stiff-necked to handle a mallet, she allowed herself to be persuaded to try how she could get on,—which is all rather ridiculous, when you remember that at the Churchills' last week she played against young Churchill, who is one of the best players, and beat him."

"Well, it does not much matter, after all," said Julia. "No one is taken in by her little tricks."

"Indeed, they are," remonstrated Ellen. "I am sure Mr. Wentworth was thoroughly impressed with Minnie's un-worldliness, for he took much trouble to teach her."

"But Mr. Wentworth is far too clever to be deceived so easily," put in Charlotte.

"Oh, nonsense!" cried Ellen. "A curate can be hoodwinked as well as any other man; and you can make him out as much of a saint as you like, Charlotte, but you can't deny that your saint is a man, and plays croquet, which is very earthly indeed."

At this moment a click of the garden gate was heard.

"Why, who can that be?" said Hester.

Ellen burst into a laugh. "Why, look at Julia, Hester. It's William, of course."

Julia lowered her eyes, and bore the laughter complacently, somewhat proud of her lover's assiduity; but Effie, who had started forward to glance from the open window, exclaimed delightedly to her father, who had roused himself from his persistent study of the *Times*, "Papa, papa; it's Philip!"

The expression of the sisters' countenances altered somewhat. Julia's face fell considerably, while Effie looked positively radiant, as she ran from the room to greet the new arrival at the street door. She returned presently, however, followed by Philip Royle, and some seconds passed before the kissing and hand-shaking consequent upon his appearance were over. At last he stretched himself into an armchair, with a muttered expression of fatigue.

"Did you come from Hampshire this morning?" asked his father.

"Yes; I left there by an early train," answered Philip; and as he spoke there came to his mind a vision of the serious, beautiful face that had been turned to him only that morning, and that formed such a contrast to the smooth, fair prettiness of his sisters.

"I suppose you have enjoyed yourself immensely, and seen a sight of people?" asked his father again.

"Yes; I have seen a number of persons," returned Philip. "I have stayed at house after house, and I met several fellows there whom I had known at Oxford. You have heard me speak of Gilbert Jocelyn, with whom I was very intimate at one time, also at the university? He was staying at Lyndwood with some friends, and he was very cordial and pleasant."

There was a brief silence; and then Philip Royle, looking across to his third sister, said, with a smile, "I have not seen you, Julia, since your new honours have come upon you, have I? But I hope you had my letter of congratulation. I don't remember Dawson very well. You see, I have been so little at home of late; but I know how highly I have heard him eulogised by you all, and I am sure I wish you every happiness."

"Philip does make such wonderful speeches," laughed Ellen; "they are like the phrases of the gentlemen of title in the *London Journal* stories."

"He's right enough, Ellen," said Mr.

Royle. "He has to talk like that when he's among his grand friends, and he ought to keep up the habit. What was the use of his going to Oxford, if the masters there didn't teach him how to talk?"

His father's tone and words jarred inexpressibly upon Philip's quick ear.

"I spoke naturally," he said, turning to Ellen, "and I certainly did not go out of my way to be ungrammatical."

The entrance of Mr. William Dawson, whose step upon the gravel walk in front of the house, and whose mild ring, had not been heard, put a stop to the discussion. The new-comer was not an acquisition. He was a type of the young man who is invariably described by friends as a really very gentlemanly person. He was well dressed, and he was by no means bad looking, yet the most undiscerning critic could not fail to observe that the true gold of Dawson's character was largely mixed with the alloy of plebeian origin and surroundings. No amount of polish would have brightened him, no intelligent companionship would have brought out his refined qualities of mind; he was a rough diamond, a very rough diamond! Philip wondered again and again that evening, as he looked at his sister and her lover, how such a betrothal could have come about. The pair seemed so unequally gifted. She was pretty and "ladylike," and even somewhat refined in her tastes and ideas; he was good-tempered and good-hearted, but the wildest friendly

enthusiasm could not attribute refinement to him in any shape or measure.

He entered the room on the evening
in question, like a hurricane; he gave
his betrothed a loud, reverberating kiss,
and he wrung Philip's hand, on being
introduced to him formally, and clapped
him on the shoulder, exclaiming, "I've
met you before, old boy, at one or
another of the tea-fights that have taken
place in the neighbourhood. You may
not remember me, but I remember you,
and I am glad to meet you again under
these pleasant circumstances. We shall
be great chums, I'm sure, in the future,
and needn't be troubled by any questions
of pride or prejudice, you know. Whoever has the tin stands the drink, is
my motto."

"I will bear your precept in mind," returned Philip, smiling; "and I trust fate will not compel me to make too many thirsty attacks on your purse."

"Oh, we shall shuffle along famously, I've no doubt," declared Mr. Dawson. So saying, he seated himself near the future Mrs. Dawson, who was striving to appear ignorant of, and totally indifferent to, his vicinity.

There was a silence, presently interrupted by Mr. Dawson, who exclaimed with a laugh, "I say, this is a Quaker's meeting, and no mistake. Governor, why don't you say something? Are you not pleased to have the chip of the old block home again, or has he come to say his allowance isn't large enough?"

"That's none of your business, my

boy, any way," said Mr. Royle, good-humouredly. "Of course, I am glad to see him—he knows that well enough; and even if he had outrun his allowance, I'm not the man to grumble at him. Young men will be young men."

"Yes, and old men will be old men, that's the worst of it!" observed Mr. Dawson. "If all governors had your principles, I shouldn't object to them; but they mostly have a very different way of thinking. I know mine kept me very close indeed until I went into the business with him. Now, of course, I have as much as I want; and I have to work for it too, I can tell you! The governor is down on you like a knife, if he thinks you don't keep up the steam. However, I don't mind that. It's right and fair enough that a man should work for his living; all I want is a fair day's wage for a fair day's work, as our men say when they come grumbling to me."

The words struck upon Philip's susceptible organization; he gave no outward sign of the sting, however, and asked Mr. Dawson, with perfect calmness, "May I ask what is your special sphere?"

"Soap," was Dawson's laconic reply.

"Not soft soap, I hope," said Philip.

"Not I. No," said young Dawson; "I leave that for your fine friends. We go in for soap-boiling. Dawson and Son is one of the biggest soap-boiling concerns in the country, and brings in a pretty sum of money too—my share of which your sister's going to help me spend, aren't you, July?"

"I don't know what she will do," remarked Ellen, "but she says she is going to be wonderfully prudent, to manage and put by, and make both ends meet, and all sorts of other dreadful things."

"I dare say I shall contrive to spend quite as much as William will think necessary, after a year or so," said Julia.

"What's the matter with Eff?" inquired young Dawson, as his roving eye fell upon the face of his youngest future sister-in-law. "She looks as languishing as a dying duck, doesn't she, governor?"

The "governor" laughed, and Charlotte said, somewhat scornfully, "Oh, she is in rapt adoration of Philip—that's all."

"Something like your adoration of Wentworth, eh?" retorted Dawson.

Then he added, turning to Philip, "Do you know Wentworth? No, I can see you do not. Well, he is a Ritualist curate, and the womankind in this neighbourhood are wild about him. The fact is, he is rather good-looking, and contrives to look very pale and to have dark circles round his eyes, you know—I wouldn't swear that he doesn't paint. Then he gets himself up in a sort of military clerical style, with sashes round his waist, and gold chains with crosses and medals round his neck, and a crucifix hanging by a long chain at his side, I believe; and he makes desperate love—in a clerical way, of course—to every woman he sees, and asks them all to work for the Church; so the result is that they send him in bales of embroidery for altar-cloths, and I'm told he's going to have a bazaar and dispose of the pairs of slippers sent him, for the benefit of the parish. Charlotte is working him a smoking-cap, I was told."

Charlotte had left the room while he was speaking, at which he was infinitely amused.

"Do you admire the curate, Effie?" asked her brother, turning to the gentle girl beside him, who had not spoken since his arrival.

"I don't mind him," she replied, with evident indifference as to the subject; and added immediately, "but you haven't said how long you will be in town, Philip. I am afraid you will be going off again somewhere, and I shall not see you for months."

" Have you secured any invitations for the next month or two ? " asked Mr. Royle, addressing his son.

Philip's face flushed painfully as he replied, " Yes ; one or two persons have been kind enough to press me to visit them. I hardly know, however, which house I care to favour."

"I should pretty soon make up my mind," said young Dawson. " Where there are the prettiest girls and the best feeding is the place for me. That's why I drop in here so often, isn't it, governor ? "

" Philip professes not to notice the ladies," said Ellen. " He never will tell us anything about his grand friends —how they are dressed, and how they behave. Now, if William went to a ball at the house of some lord or lady, he would have a wonderful string of things to tell."

Mr. Dawson, having protested that all girls were " tarred with the same brush," begged Julia to take a turn round the garden with him, and listen to a full exposition of his views; and when the pair had gone to walk backwards and forwards along the gravel walk beneath the window, Philip inquired—

"Where did Julia pick up this young man ? "

" She's met him at different houses in the neighbourhood," replied Mr. Royle. "The elder Dawson is a very rich man, I can tell you, and young William is not a match to be despised. He is a partner in the business, and has a handsome income as it is; and, of course, when the old gentleman dies, he will be master of the whole place, and will have a position not to be sneezed at, if I know anything of the matter."

"But does Julia care for him?" said Philip.

"Oh, she likes him very well. Why shouldn't she?" responded her father. "He's as kind as he can be to her, and makes himself at home with us; and, then, all the girls in the parish have tried to get him, I'm told, and Julia's proud of her success. Altogether, I think she's made a very fair hit, and I don't complain."

"You see, we have not all been used to the society of aristocrats," said Ellen, with some asperity, "and are not above the level of William Dawson."

"I am sorry to hear it," was Philip's sole reply.

And in a moment he rose to leave, promising his sister Effie, who accompanied him to the gate, that he would come again very soon.

CHAPTER VI.

PHILIP ROYLE walked back to his chambers in Regent Street, in deep thought. His position was by no means a pleasant one, and it was not strange that it annoyed him considerably. His father, a wholesale tea-dealer of great repute in the City, had had but one idea, one dream, one ambition. That was—to make a gentleman of his son; to send him to one of the universities; to afford him an ample allowance, that would enable him to cultivate the society of men of birth and breeding,—in short, to elevate him, to raise him from the trading class to which he naturally belonged, and, by force of money, make him appear that which he was not. The father himself had no pretensions of any kind. He was a good-hearted, outspoken man of business, who had risen from a post approaching that of an errand-boy, to be the head of the house. He had married, early in life, a woman of his own rank, who had borne him six children, and had then died; and he had never attempted to draw himself and his wife and daughters from the sphere which was natural to him. But for his son his ambition was immeasurable, and he looked to him for the realization of brilliant dreams of social supremacy—of refined and cultivated intercourse with men and women of a higher world than that to which a tradesman could aspire. While other men of his class looked to their sons to carry on their business when they were gone, he had simply a keen desire to put his son out of the pale of commerce ; and nothing pleased him so much as when a City friend said, casually—

" Your son has made some grand friends, and goes into fashionable society, I'm told."

Of course, all the friends and acquaintances of the Royles were in a perpetual state of indignation at the father's presumption and the son's want of spirit, and very sharp things were said about the whole family, when they were not present. But at the same time, whenever

Philip Royle had made his appearance at any of the festive gatherings held by the various members of his father's circle of friends, the most obsequious attention had been paid him; hosts had apologized to him for their entertainments, and hostesses had asked him innumerable questions relating to his previous experience among the " high and mighty " of the land.

The wives and daughters and sisters of Mr. Royle's many City friends were better disposed towards Philip than the men; being women, they could assimilate themselves, better than could men, with the superior tone and manner of Philip's bearing. As is always the case, the women were far more cultivated than men of their own rank, and did not feel out of their element in society that was intolerably irksome to the stronger sex. Then, Philip was handsome, had a certain distinction of appearance that is always attractive, and knew how to make himself irresistibly agreeable if he wished; therefore it was not surprising that he was well received by his father's friends, and also well abused by them when he was not present.

The young man was undoubtedly in a very unsatisfactory position. He had been brought up almost like the son of an aristocrat; he had taken his degree at Oxford; he had subsequently achieved a short tour on the Continent; and he had, on his return, installed himself, at his father's desire, in some handsome rooms in Regent Street. The greater number of young men would have been, of course, delighted at such a condition of affairs, would have revelled in the ample allowance and unbroken leisure, and would have laughed at any ideas of duty or dignity. But Philip Royle had something in him beyond the average comprehension, and his anomalous footing in London society was a constant worry to him. Since he had known Silvia Clevedon, his feelings on the point had become even stronger. He had met her several times at Lyndwood, and had been greatly impressed, not only by her beauty, but by her originality of thought and simple frankness of speech. He had heard her explaining several broad principles in a half-serious, half-jocular manner, and he had felt convinced that she would be very severe on him could she know his story. Yet what was he to do? He could not, in return for his father's great kindness, run counter to his dearest wishes; and, at the same time, he could not make up his mind to spend his life in thorough inaction.

"My father was wrong," he muttered to himself, as he entered his luxurious rooms on the evening of his return, "to bring me up as he has done. He has given me ideas 'above my station;' whereas, if I had grown to manhood after the manner of young Dawson, I should have been far happier. I should never have seen Miss Clevedon, and could not have wasted my time thinking of her, therefore." And he lit a

cigar and flung himself into a chair by
the window, and went over once again
in his mind that morning's interlude
among the ferns of the Hampshire
forest.

It was some three or four days after
Philip Royle's departure from Lyndwood,
that as Silvia and Gilbert Jocelyn were
out on the shady lawn at the back of
Clevedon House in the afternoon, Jocelyn
exclaimed suddenly, after a long pause,
during which he had watched Silvia's
face—

"Now then, Silvia, what's the matter?
you look as solemn as an Englishman
out for a holiday. Why so wan and
pale, sweet Silvia?—if Suckling will
excuse my rather free version of his
line."

"I was thinking of Mr. Royle, to tell the truth," said Silvia, somewhat absently.

"I should not have believed you capable of such waste of thought," replied Jocelyn. "Did you light upon him by accident, or is it a confirmed bad habit?"

"The thought came naturally enough," said Silvia. "It struck me just now how idle and contemptible we both were—you and I, I mean—sitting here in the fresh, cool air, out of the reach of the sun, with nothing to do, nothing to trouble us, nothing to grieve us; while men and women, and even children, are working so hard in this hot weather, all over the country, for miserable sums of money that would hardly keep our dogs. Then

I thought of the immense self-satisfaction of honourable work. That is how he came to my mind."

"I don't see the connection, I confess," said Jocelyn, opening his eyes wide at Silvia's last remark. "If there be one thing specially antipathetic to Royle, I should say it is work in any shape or form."

"I should have thought so too," said Silvia, "but for a few words he said when I met him the other morning."

"Did you have a talk with him, then?" inquired Jocelyn, looking eagerly at his companion.

"Yes, he walked beside me for a few moments," said Silvia, quite calmly and frankly; "and he said, among other things, that he should have liked to have spoken to me on the question of work."

"By-the-by, he said something to me on the subject, the last time I met him at the Eagle," remarked Jocelyn.

"Evidently there is some thought in his mind," began Silvia."

"My dear Silvia," said Jocelyn, impatiently, "the man's struck by your fine eyes, and he thinks that he can win you by appealing to you for guidance and help. Women are always amenable to that sort of flattery."

Silvia took up a book that lay on the chair beside her, and said quietly, "If you are bent on that conventional style of jocularity, I would rather read than listen to you. You know, nothing vexes me more than the absurd habit of presupposing that a young man cannot look at a girl without falling in love."

Jocelyn laughed, saying, "Put your book down, Silvia; I will be perfectly sensible. And do tell me what Royle said when you met him out in the forest in the early morning."

"He said nothing very remarkable," Silvia proceeded. "As I told you, he wanted to talk about work, and I did not encourage him, for I did not care to enter into any discussion on any subject with him. You know, he did not impress me pleasantly from the first. Still, he seemed excited and disturbed the other morning."

"Perhaps he had been drinking hard overnight," suggested Jocelyn.

Silvia continued, without heeding the

interruption, "And I have thought of it several times since, and have been sorry that I did not allow him to talk. There may have been a germ of good in the man's nature, which I have utterly trodden down."

"As to that," said Jocelyn, lazily, "I always thought there was something in the fellow worth attention, in spite of his wildness. But you women always contrive to stifle the good in a man, somehow; and you see even such a superior and thoroughly well-intentioned bit of womanhood as yourself is not free from the failing. You have an opportunity of impressing and improving Royle, and, by Jove! the only use you make of your chance is to snub him."

Silvia listened the with utmost gravity,

and there was a pained expression on her face when Jocelyn ceased speaking.

"Perhaps you are right," she murmured; "perhaps I did lose an opportunity of doing some good. I am very sorry for it."

"Well, I don't think it much matters in the long run," said Jocelyn. "You are not likely to have kept him from going to the bad. It would want a powerful influence to have that effect on Royle; and therefore, since he must go there, it's of little importance how soon he goes."

"Why will you talk in that absurd style?" said Silvia, turning quickly upon Jocelyn. "One would think, to hear you, that you believed what you said. To begin with, you are altogether wrong. It matters greatly to me whether or not any one 'goes to the bad,' as you put it; and you said a moment ago, yourself, that I had an opportunity of impressing Mr. Royle; and, finally, I entirely dispute your theory that it's of little importance how soon he goes."

"At all events, we won't discuss the matter, because we shall inevitably quarrel, and I don't like quarrelling with ladies," said Jocelyn.

"And they might get the better of you," remarked Silvia. "At any rate, when you see Mr. Royle, you might tell him, Gilbert——"

"Oh, come—— No," said Jocelyn, his face reddening and his brow clouding; "I am not going to act as a go-between. What you have to say to Royle, you can say to him; he will greatly prefer that, and so shall I."

For all answer, Silvia took up her book with a smile of evident amusement on her face, and went on reading for some moments, while Jocelyn was fuming at his own absurdity. Presently he said—

"Never mind my exclamation just now, Silvia; tell me what you wish me to say to Mr. Royle."

Silvia laughed as she caught Jocelyn's eye, and merely replied, "Never mind the message, Gilbert. Since you are so squeamish, I will find some less inflammable means of letting Mr. Royle know that I sympathize with his desire to work. And now you had better leave me to my book, and go to the Eagle and flirt. The pretty Miss Ramsdens are there, I'm told, so you will be in your element."

With these words, Silvia called to her

dog, and, book in hand, walked leisurely along the smooth lawn towards the conservatory, her soft white drapery forming a line of light behind her.

The result of this conversation was that when Jocelyn went up to London for a day a fortnight later, and met Royle in Bond Street, he fairly astounded him by exclaiming—

"I say, Royle, I have a message for you from Miss Clevedon."

"For me?" cried Royle.

"Well, that is to say," proceeded Jocelyn, "I ought to have a message, but I haven't, because a little discussion arose just as she was about to give it, so that it was never delivered to me. The fact remains, however, that she had a message for you."

"But don't you know what it was about?" said Royle, eagerly.

"Something about work and independence, and those unpleasant kind of subjects that Miss Clevedon particularly favours, I'm certain," said Jocelyn; "for she was talking about them at the time with her usual enthusiasm. She said I ought to be ashamed of myself for sitting on the lawn enjoying a smoke in the shade, while hundreds of men and women and children were working hard. Really, I am very sorry if they are working harder than is good for them, but I don't see that I can do anything to help them. However, Miss Clevedon would have an answer ready, I have no doubt."

"When is the family coming to town?" asked Royle.

"Very soon—in a few weeks," said Jocelyn; "so you will be able to discuss these terrible affairs at length; and I should think you had better grind yourself to the level of the extraordinarily democratic theories you will be treated to. Good-bye; I shall see you soon. I'll look you up when we come to town."

And, with a nod and a smile, Jocelyn passed on.

"I've made it all right, Silvia," said Jocelyn, a few hours later, as he sat at the Clevedons' dinner-table, some eighty or ninety miles from the great metropolis. "I met Royle by accident in London to-day, and I told him that the divine light of genius was about to shine on him, in the shape of admonitions from you on man's sphere of work."

"What nonsense of Silvia's is that?" asked the admiral, glancing keenly down the table.

"It is merely a question of conversion, sir," replied Jocelyn. "Silvia thinks every one should work—that every man should use his brains."

"No, I do not," replied Silvia; "for I know that some men have none."

The admiral interposed here—"Leave the matter in peace, for the present; I will not have any discussions over the dinner-table."

And the admiral was obeyed.

CHAPTER VII.

SILVIA CLEVELAND only deepened the impression she had made upon Philip Royle, when, late in the autumn, she was back in London with her father and mother, and settled for the winter in the town house. They met frequently, and met in a more informal manner than if the season had been in full swing, with its never-ending dissipations, its ceaseless conventionalities, its formalities and restrictions. There were pleasant gatherings of intimate friends; there were unceremonious small dinners; there were afternoon teas in the firelight; there were expeditions to theatres, concerts, and picture-galleries;—there were innumerable opportunities, in short, for developing an acquaintance, and discovering excellencies and failings of character, that could not be discerned at first sight. Silvia and Royle had many long conversations amid the laughter and gossip around them. They talked on serious subjects, and on subjects light as air'; they discussed politics, art, music, literature ; they fought several severe battles over abstruse theories, and metaphorically dealt each other some hard blows. Silvia was greatly amused and interested by Royle, and keenly enjoyed a controversy with him;

and Royle himself was in a curious state
of mind, which he did not stop to
examine. Silvia had given a sudden
turn to all his thoughts and ideas. He
found himself meditating on subjects to
which he had not given a moment's
reflection before he knew her; he found
himself to be strongly interested in
questions on which, only a year ago,
he would have yawned unceasingly. He
was astonished sometimes to discover
how completely he was changing; how
he no longer liked the same books, the
same scenes, the same amusements; how
involuntarily, as it seemed to Royle,
the books Silvia praised crept into his
book-case; how he lingered longest by
the pictures he had heard her admire;
how he gradually deserted Bond Street,

and Regent Street, and Piccadilly, his old parade ground, and found himself walking and thinking in very unfashionable by-ways, at times. He caught himself wandering now and then amid the terrible squalor and misery of St. Giles's, noting the haggard faces, the bruised and cut features, the unkempt hair of the poor people crowding about the courts and alleys; noting, with an eye grown keener of late, the narrow, dark doorways, the reeking cellars, the indescribably squalid aspect of the hideous tumble-down houses that form the homes of the poor; noting the careworn expression of the young children, the hopeless dreariness of the pale women sitting on the doorsteps nursing the hapless babies. And in the midst of such scenes

he could not help asking himself sometimes what he had done to deserve his
happier fate.

Yes; Royle was certainly growing
more serious, and at the same time he
was growing less discontented. At one
moment he had been inclined to believe,
as many young men do, that fate was
against him; that the whole creation
had entered upon a deliberate plan to
keep him in the background; that the
ruling powers of the earth, the heavens,
and all space combined to concoct a
device for his displacement at a supper-
table! Now, however, the perception
was coming upon him that he was
undeservedly fortunate; and this new
humility softened and improved him.

Men are, for the most part, unobservant,

especially of each other, and Royle's companions did not appear to notice his alteration; but his sisters were quick to see a difference in him, and a few brisk controversies were held on the subject at Laurel Lodge. Royle's youngest sister, Effie, ventured once to make some gentle remark to him respecting the change she saw in him; but he only answered, lightly—

"Changed, am I, Effie? Well, I hope it's for the better."

And when Effie whispered her thoughts about Philip to her father, as she sat in her customary place by his armchair at night, Mr. Royle only laughed and pinched his daughter's ear, saying—

"He's in love, Eff, take my word for it."

But Effie answered, thoughtfully, "No, papa; I don't think it is that."

Mr. Royle was not, to tell the truth, quite satisfied with his son lately. He had shown symptoms of a growing distaste to his anomalous position in society; he did not enter at all readily into his father's schemes for his advancement; and he had even said, in so many words, that he was tired of his idle life, and wanted to work. Now, to Mr. Royle, idleness was the distinctive mark of the gentleman; directly a man worked he became a trader and a vulgarian. He was consequently very irate at these faint indications of a latent spirit in his son, and, had it not been for a lingering hope that the ideas were but transient, would have had an angry explanation of the first mild show of independence. He had told his daughter that Philip was surely in love, but he did not really believe it—"for," he said to himself, "love doesn't make you anxious to work, or fond of your books, that ever I heard of. It simply makes most youngsters lose all chances of success, and throw prudence and prosperity to the dogs, for the sake of a nod and a wink from a pretty doll, who's only waiting till your back is turned to give a nod and a wink to another fellow. That's my idea of love, and that's not what is the matter with Philip."

Perhaps, if Mr. Royle could have seen his son at the various entertainments honoured by Miss Clevedon's presence, he might have imagined that love, like disease, does not attack all alike.

The machinery that was to completely overthrow Mr. Royle's elaborate fabric was set in motion, finally, one December night. Philip Royle had been asked to join a few friends at an unceremonious gathering in the pretty rooms of a Kensington mansion, and the moment he entered the principal room to pay his respects to the hostess, that lady pounced upon him, and said eagerly—

"I am so glad to see you, Mr. Royle, and I want to ask you a particular favour."

"Anything that is within human power I will do my utmost to effect for you," said Royle.

"Oh, it's nothing very dreadful," returned Mrs. Ormond, hurriedly; then, lowering her voice, and looking round the room as if in search of some one, she continued, "The fact is, there's a young lady here to-night who is said to be very clever, and very peculiar, too, and I really don't know what to do with her. Nobody has spoken to her, I'm afraid, and I am sure I don't know what to say to her, or I would do it. But people seem in awe of her, and although she is so beautiful, the young men have kept carefully away. Now, you would oblige me so very much if you would just devote yourself to her for a few moments."

Royle smiled. "I am ready for the sacrifice," he answered. "Who is the lady?"

"Miss Clevedon, the daughter of Admiral Clevedon, and——"

Mrs. Ormond was entering into a detailed account of the Clevedon family, from which Royle diverted her by exclaiming—

"I know Miss Clevedon very well, and am glad to find she is here. I will go and devote myself to her according to directions."

And, with a bow to his relieved hostess, Royle went off in search of Silvia, stopping once or twice to award the usual civilities to people he knew. At last he reached her, and he had the satisfaction of seeing her face brighten at his approach. She was sitting on a sofa in an isolated part of the room, in the shade of two sturdy indiarubber plants, that stood in huge pots in the recess of the window, and when

Royle's eye first fell upon her, she was looking somewhat downcast. As, however, he stepped across the room to take the place beside her, her face was lit up by a welcoming smile, and she exclaimed—

"I was thinking just now what an opportunity this would be for one of our violent discussions, and you have appeared in answer to my thought. I had no idea, however, that you knew Mrs. Ormond."

"I have known her for a long time," he answered, simply.

Then they were both silent for a time, Silvia looking indolently at the people flitting about her, Royle watching her; and suddenly an idea came to him, an idea which swiftly became a firm resolution, and before reason could in-

terfere to prevent him, he murmured—
"Miss Clevedon, will you listen to me
for a few moments?"

"Certainly," said Silvia, turning round
to him with her brightest smile. "I only
claim the privilege of stopping you when
I have heard enough. What are you
going to say? You look very serious."

"And yet I hardly know why I should
ask you to listen," said Royle, in a low
voice. "It is some impulse that seems
forcing me to speak."

"I am glad of that," said Silvia; "I
like people to speak from impulse."

Encouraged by that sentence, Royle
began, speaking still in a low voice, and
fixing his eyes earnestly on Silvia's face.
"You will think, I am sure," he said,
"that I am the most selfish fellow alive,

to want to confide my troubles to you; but the truth is, that you have already been so kind to me in listening to my opinions, and in expressing to me your own, that I feel it impossible to be on a false footing with you, whom I respect and admire before all the world. I want you, at least, to know me truly as I am."

"But I very much object to that idea of yours of telling the truth to one person only," said Silvia. "Every one should know you truly as you are."

"I know, I know," rejoined Royle; "and, believe me, I was not the originator of my own false position. Miss Clevedon, you must have heard numberless remarks and criticisms and suspicions respecting me in the society to which you were born. I have heard them indirectly myself."

"It was in your power to put aside all that was said, if you were prepared to tell the truth," said Silvia.

"The thing is," replied Royle, "that until lately I had no particular aspirations. I did not care much, I think, whether or no my position were a false one. I felt discontented with myself generally, but on no praiseworthy grounds. Now, if I have got one or two better ideas, they are due to you. You have taught me to feel that the world is something more than a mere playground; you have made me feel that independence of action and intellect are within reach, and that no man has a right to waste his life."

"If it is true that I have brought you to this," said Silvia, "I have achieved

something worth achieving. It is difficult, as a rule, to make a man realize his
own shortcomings."

"And now," continued Royle, earnestly, "I want a few words of encouragement from you before I determine
on action. I have never been heard to
make any reference to my family, it is
said; but I am going to make a full
confession to you. My family is not an
aristocratic one, and I have no place,
by right, in the society I frequent, so
that the world's suppositions are, in some
cases, truths. My father is a wholesale
tea-merchant—— Don't laugh, Miss
Clevedon," he exclaimed, as she bent her
head over the flowers she held.

But, as his appeal fell upon her ear,
she raised her eyes gravely to his face,

and protested, "I had no idea of laughing, Mr. Royle. I only wish there were nothing worse than tea-dealing among our aristocratic families."

"I know I am pulling my position to pieces," said Royle, hurriedly, "but it's true. My father is a tea-merchant, and would only be tolerated, for instance, in these rooms to-night because of his money. I have five sisters and no brothers; and I being the only son, my father resolved, before I was old enough to have any will in the matter, that I should not be sullied by trade—that I should be made a thorough gentleman, with a gentleman's education, a gentleman's tastes, and a gentleman's friends. He did everything he could for me; he sent me to college, he supplied me libe-

rally with money, and when I had taken
my degree and left the place, he took
chambers for me in Regent Street, and
encouraged me to spend as much money
as he thought necessary to a gentleman's
position. That style of life amused me
at first. I got on well. My college
friends were very kind to me, and asked
me to their homes, and I was introduced
to their sisters and cousins, and my poor
father was proud and delighted. But I
soon grew tired of it all, and soon realized
that men wondered why I never asked
them to my home—why they never met
my sisters and cousins. When I met
you at Lyndwood, you made me feel that
there is one thing that money cannot
buy—that is, intellect. I admired your
independence of mind and your original

opinions from the first, and I assure you that you began my regeneration. Lately my present position has become hateful to me. I want to make myself a name, if I can. I want to work; I want to win an honourable place in public opinion by my talents, rather than by money. I am tired of false pretences; I want to tell the world my real position. In short, I am anxious to let the truth come uppermost. Surely you will sympathize with me, and encourage me, will you not?"

"I sympathize with you fully," said Silvia, "but I think you have planned a most difficult course for yourself. If you intend to tell society at large that which you have just told me, I am afraid it will be a severe test for many persons whom you believe to be your friends."

"You think people will throw me over?" asked Royle.

"I am afraid so," Silvia replied. Then she added, "You know, the average men and women we meet haven't many ideas or scruples respecting duty, and honour, and dignity. They keep right involuntarily. They do not steal or murder, because it's not the habit in their social circle, and because they are rarely, if ever, strongly tempted. But they do not understand the refinement of feeling that makes a man scruple to waste the money he has not earned, and they would be utterly unable to comprehend the high ground you take. These people will, one and all, when they find you determined not to spend in idleness the money for which your father has worked hard, believe you to be an Utopist and an enthusiast, and will systematically avoid you. You haven't told me what work you have thought of trying."

"I have made no plans," said Royle. "I am fit for nothing, Miss Clevedon. In spite of my college training, I find myself utterly bewildered when there is a question of earning my own living. You see, all my life long I have been told, first and foremost, to learn to be a gentleman."

"Some men never learn the lesson to the end of their days!" remarked Silvia. "That is a question of nature, not of learning, and I don't think any amount of observant study of other people's habits and manners will correct an ungentlemanly nature."

"You are right, doubtless," muttered Royle, "and I don't stop to draw any personal conclusion from your words, because I dread the result. You have already told me how I fall short of your ideal gentleman, on the occasion of a cricket-match below the Bench at Lynd-wood, and I do not wish to call down any further blame from you. For days past, I have been thinking of confiding my doubts and perplexities to you, and have put off the confession day by day, always half afraid of the result. I did not think you would henceforth 'cut' me because of my father's position, but because of my own aimless, ignoble sort of life. I never intended, however, to venture on the question to-night, and you must forgive me for choosing such an inappropriate occasion."

"It is all very painful," said Silvia, slowly and thoughtfully, her eyes still bent upon her flowers, and her restless fingers busy among the delicate buds and leaves.

"What is it that is painful?" asked Royle.

"The whole of your story," said Silvia. "For your life so far will have been wasted."

"Hardly that," answered Royle, with a smile. "If I may count upon your genuine friendship, the gain far out-balances the loss."

"I wish I could hope that you would keep all your present friends through this crisis in your life," said Silvia; "but you seem to have made few real friends, Mr. Royle, and only deep and sincere friendship can stand such a test. Of course, it is far more honourable to you that you should make your own name and fame unaided. It is far more creditable that you should refuse to fritter away your father's earnings on idle follies, than that you should linger on in discontent, and falsehood, and dependence. I naturally admire a man who has made his own way, who has carved his own path to fame from a modest starting-point, far more than the man who wins a high place backed by influence, money, friends, and natural position. A man who rises from the ranks is doubly a hero: he is a hero because of his genius, and he is a hero because of his steadfast perseverance and defiance of temptations. That is my opinion, at least; and you will find that few people agree with me, I am afraid."

"If many women thought as you do, Miss Clevedon," said Royle, "men might be better than they are. But, as yet, women generally prevent men improving themselves in any way except in that which brings in money. When I am imbued with some honourable ambition, when I have finally settled upon the career that will lead me to fame, may I confide my hopes and aspirations to you, Miss Clevedon?"

"Certainly, if the confidence can do you any good," replied Silvia.

"And you will try to sympathize with

me?" pleaded Royle, his voice growing more and more earnest, and even impassioned. "You will remember that you are responsible for the change that has come over me; and when I have dropped out of your world by reason of my poverty and my determination to be independent, you will think of me sometimes, and wish me every success, will you not?"

"Most heartily," said Silvia, gently. "And you may be sure, Mr. Royle, that if you become an honourable worker in a good cause, success will follow, and who knows but that you will reach the 'gilded pinnacle of Fame'?"

"If such a day should ever come," said Royle, in a low voice, "will you let me lay my laurels at your feet?"

Silvia looked up quickly at him, answering lightly, "It is rather premature to talk about the disposal of your laurels, before you have sown the seeds; and by the time your wreaths are green, you will have plenty of persons most willing to accept them as a tribute from you."

"Thank you, I understand the hint," said Royle, drawing himself up stiffly, and his whole aspect changing.

"Then you understand more than I mean," said Silvia, gravely. "I was giving no hint; in fact, I do not see that any hint was necessary or even possible."

Royle did not answer, and did not relax his sudden stiffness of attitude and coldness of expression. Silvia had wounded him deeply, and he showed it.

He fancied that she meant to check any advances he was inclined to make, he construed her light words into a decided repudiation, and his pride was sorely ruffled. He sat still and silent beside her, watching moodily the laughing and flirting of Mrs. Ormond's guests, and Silvia herself was lost in wonder at his strange manner.

At this stage of affairs, Mrs. Ormond's youngest daughter, a gushing young person of not more than seventeen, came up to Silvia, and taking her hand with *empressement*, said enthusiastically, " Now, dearest Miss Clevedon, we do so want you to dance just this once."

" Not a *pas seul*, I hope," said Silvia, smiling.

" How can you say such things ? "

responded Miss Ormond, with a light laugh. "No; we are going to have a waltz to please all the young people, and we do so want you to join it. I think one waltz, you know, in the middle of an evening that's not devoted to dancing, is so very exquisite, you know, just to remind one of gaiety, and enjoyment, and all that sort of thing. All the girls are going to join in, and you must not refuse. Mr. Royle, do try and persuade her. There, mamma is playing that divine waltz of Strauss's, 'Nachtfalter,' and I shall set off dancing all by myself, if I don't go back to my partner."

And, with a nod and a smile, and a final pressure of Silvia's hand, Miss Ormond hurried away.

"Will you dance this waltz with me,

then?" said Royle, turning coldly towards Silvia.

"Certainly not," replied Silvia, "if you do not wish it."

He laughed an odd, bitter laugh, saying, "If I do not wish it? You know the world better than that, Miss Clevedon. It is rather a question of condescension on your part."

"There is no such thing as condescension between friends," said Silvia.

Royle's whole face brightened.

"Thanks for that thought," he said heartily; and, starting to his feet, he held out his hand towards Silvia, saying, "You must take at least a few turns with me."

As they stood side by side, watching for a moment or two before they began, Royle remarked, "I have never yet danced with you."

"No," said Silvia, as if she did not remember the fact; "perhaps not. I very seldom dance; it is so tiring, and I do not enjoy it at all, as a rule. I agree with the Shah of Persia, who preferred to have it all done for him, and I am quite contented to lie on my cushions and smoke my hookah—metaphorically, of course—and watch the dancers."

They took a few turns only, and then Silvia protested that it tired her, and sank back into a chair. She looked constrained and even disturbed, and did not glance at Royle, as he stood beside her in wonder at her discomposure—she who was generally so calm and collected, and thoroughly at ease.

"I am really very tired," she said at

last; "I wish you would take me through these rooms to my mother. I dare say she is ready to go."

When they had found Mrs. Clevedon, that lady declared in an undertone that she was dying to go, and Royle accompanied them to the carriage door. As he leant in at the window to say good night to them, Silvia said—

"Don't forget our conversation, Mr. Royle, and remember that plain, honest truth is better than the best gilded lie!"

"I shall not forget, you may be sure," he replied.

Nor did he.

CHAPTER VIII.

IT was on the Saturday after his conversation with Silvia at the Ormonds', that Philip Royle went up to Laurel Lodge early in the afternoon, in order to have an explanation with his father. The City house being closed at one o'clock on that day, he knew that Mr. Royle would be at home, according to his custom, and that he could get through the dreaded interview before dinner-time came and precluded a private conversation.

It was with a curious mixture of feelings that he made his way through the leafless desert of Regent's Park. He was at a loss to understand his own action, and caught himself wondering every now and then why he should not be as idle as his father wished him to be, and lead as tranquil and unambitious a life as that his father indicated. But something within him had changed. He felt that he could not now settle down to the indolent enjoyment of previous years; he wanted some firm standpoint, some resolute aim, some ennobling hope. He was no longer content to saunter through life; he wanted to stride boldly forward, and leave his "footprints on the sands of time." "What is it that has changed me?" he asked himself again and again. "Miss Clevedon has lectured me, and taught me to look at things in a different light, it is true; but surely that cannot have done it all."

So lost was he in his reflections on this particular day, that he reached his father's house mechanically, never having noticed the chilly, gloomy roads by which he had come; and the first thing that really roused him was the servant's volunteered information, when she had opened the door to him, that Mr. Royle was in the library.

Royle turned instantly to the small back-room dignified by the term "library," and which was, in fact, merely an un-official counting-house, where Mr. Royle cogitated on those terrible laws of supply and demand, and kept complicated accounts. His father was stretched on a sofa by the fireside, and Effie was close beside, reading the daily paper to him. As Royle entered the room, she dropped the paper, and almost screamed with delight, as she ran to put her arms round his neck.

"Oh, Philip, you are good to have come so early," she said.

"Am I, dear?" he answered. "I came up now in order to have a talk with my father before dinner."

"Very well, very well; tell me what's up," said Mr. Royle, good-humouredly. "Do you want more money?"

"No, sir; on the contrary, I want no more at all, at any time," said Royle. "Don't run away, Effie," he murmured, catching his sister's hand as she was about to leave the room.

She came back to her place then, and listened to her brother with a strange glow of pride and satisfaction at her heart.

"Now, tell me straight out what you mean," said Mr. Royle, hastily. "I'm not one of your fine folks, and don't want the sense of a thing smothered in grand talk. Say what you've got to say as plainly as you can—the plainer the better."

And Mr. Royle settled himself more comfortably among the sofa cushions, as if preparing for a long story. He glanced inquisitively at his son at the same time, wondering what was coming.

"I have not much to say," said Philip, looking frankly and fully into his father's face. "I am afraid, however, that it

will be very displeasing to you. Still,
the truth must out, displeasing or not;
and, in this case, the truth is simply that
I cannot live on in idleness and ease any
longer. I feel more and more ashamed of
it all day by day. It is dishonourable for
me, as a young, strong man, to spend
your money, the money for which you
work, in mere amusement. I know that
you do not complain; that you have
given me as much money as I thought
I wanted, without a word of reproach;
but you have been too kind to me, and
it is I who must complain at last. I
don't feel easy or happy as things are at
present, and I want to be independent,
to try and make my own fortune."

"Well, you've taken your time to
get up all these high-flown notions,"

said Mr. Royle, curtly. "In fact, the spurt is so sudden that I might have thought you had fallen in love, except for the fact that no woman has taught you all those ideas. They like a fortune ready-made to their hand far better than any questions of making one's own fortune, or of independence or honour; so I know there's no love business mixed up with your new-fangled notions. What else have you got to say?"

"I was going to say," proceeded Royle, "that it would have been better for us both if you had put me into your business when I was a boy, and had let me work steadily side by side with you at the office. I should have been straight-forward and honest then, at all events. You see, sir, a man wants something

more than money, to push him on in
good society. He wants family, and
connections, and influence. If he keep
his relations in the dark, as you have
always told me to do, people soon find
out that there is something that it is
desired to conceal, and are all the more
anxious to unearth the mystery. Most
of the men I know suspect something—
I can tell by their manner and their
hints; and sooner or later they will all
turn me a cold shoulder. Then I shall
be perfectly helpless and powerless.
Perhaps you don't realize how unsatisfactory my position often is. You don't
know how awkwardly I am placed when
a man talks to me about his home and
his family—when he introduces me to
his father and mother, and brothers and

sisters, and I do not mention mine; I introduce him to no one; I give him no invitation. All these points are difficulties that money cannot smooth. But, apart from this view, I myself feel an irresistible desire to do something for myself—to work hard in some line or another, and make money for myself. You must confess, sir, that it is not very ambitious or dignified for a son to waste his father's substance without doing his father the justice of owning him, and, however angry you may be with me, you will surely acknowledge that there is truth in what I say. I want to work my own way, I want to be of some use in the world, so that when I die it may not be said that my life has been utterly wasted. Fame is, I know, a wild and visionary ambition; but I can always hope for it, and I am sure that I should be much happier in that hope than in my present fatal certainty."

"Well, I'm blessed!" broke in Mr. Royle, in evident amazement and indignation. "If I had been told beforehand you were going to talk such nonsense, I should never have believed it. You may go on to me for weeks about independent work, but you won't make me acknowledge any of your wild schemes and plans. As for fame—— Pshaw! it makes me positively ill when I hear men raving about fame, and I never thought my own son would come to it. And what does it amount to, after all? For my part, I've found that the men who are hoping for fame, and independent name, and all that style of thing, generally are the men to throw away their luckiest cards for want of a little plain sense, and then come and borrow money. Fame means bankruptcy, as a rule. I've spent large sums of money over you, trying to make you a gentleman; and, after all this time, you come and talk to me about fame, as if you were a boy of fifteen! Pray, what are you going to work at that is to bring fame?"

"That is what I hardly know," said Royle. "That is one of the points upon which I wished to consult you. But, of course, if you will not acknowledge any good in my resolution, you will not feel inclined to discuss any plans or ideas I may have had, with me. I am determined, however, on the main point. I am a man, and I will work like a man. I don't think I should have liked to live quite idle, even if I had had an inherited fortune, as so many men I know have, and the situation is graver since you positively earn the money that I squander. Don't you understand something of what I mean, sir?"

"Pshaw! Philip," exclaimed Mr. Royle, impatiently, "you're younger than I thought you—that's all that's the matter. Young people have always got a batch of wonderful ideas about equality, and honour, and fame, and other most un-business-like sort of things. Look at Effie there; she sympathizes with all your grand notions, any one can see. But, as I've told you again and again,

I wanted to make you a gentleman; to give you the advantages of a good education, and good companions, and plenty of money; so that you might marry a real born lady, and take your place among gentlemen's families. Now, I was brought up as a tradesman, and nothing but a tradesman. My father did not trouble himself about my education much, and I was in the counting-house when I was fifteen. I've always had plenty of money, and have always been able to get most things I wanted, by money; and when you were a little chap, it struck me that I might raise the family a trifle, and trot you out a gentleman, also by the force of money. But if you prefer to starve in a garret looking out for fame, I suppose I can't prevent you. It's a pity, though, that you didn't get all these fine ideas sooner, so that a trifle of the money spent on you might have been saved."

The conversation continued for some time in this strain, Mr. Royle expressing his displeasure in unmistakably plain terms, his son exonerating himself and endeavouring to form some definite plans. But Mr. Royle was too exasperated to be able to join in any scheme for the future, and finally, just before dinner was announced, he bade his son return to talk over his affairs some other day.

"I am too much put out by all this jargon of yours about work, and honour, and so on, to attend to your suggestions now," he said, standing, as he was about to leave the room, with his hand on the handle of the door, "so you must put up with your misery for a few days more."

When his father had left the room, slamming the door after him, Philip turned curiously towards his sister. "Well, little Effie," he asked, "what do you think of it all?"

"I think you are right, of course," she answered. "You are always right, Philip."

Royle laughed at her; and it was with smiling faces that presently the brother and sister entered the dining-room together.

The dinner passed off in some constraint. Mr. Royle was not in his usual spirits, and hardly spoke at all, and his daughters could not help noticing the resentful glances he cast at his son every now and then. They asked no questions, however, and it was not until the appearance of Mr. William Dawson that any allusion was made to the evidently disturbed state of family feeling.

Julia Royle's lover came regularly every evening, about half an hour after dinner was over, and on Sundays he came to dinner. Such was the established rule with regard to the conduct of engaged young men among the Royles' friends, and he would have been a bold man who had ventured to transgress it.

Mr. Dawson had not been five minutes in the midst of his promised wife's family before he perceived that there was something wrong. He glanced keenly from the daughters to the father, and from

the father to the son, and then he
exclaimed—

"I say, governor, what's up? Has the
public found out the iron filings in your
best two-and-sixpenny, or isn't the supply
equal to the demand? There's something
wrong, I'm sure. Have you embarked
in a rotten speculation?"

"Yes; that's just about the truth of
the matter," said Mr. Royle, angrily.
"I've spent pounds and pounds of money
upon my son, and given him as much
as he wanted, and now he tells me he
wants to work for himself, to earn his
own living."

"Does he, though?" cried Dawson,
his face lighting with something like
enthusiasm. "Then, I'm excessively glad
to hear it," he exclaimed, leaning across

to Royle, and giving him an appreciative slap on the shoulder that made him wince. " I wish you every success, and you may rely on me to stand by you through thick and thin."

" William, do be quiet," said Julia, noting her father's irate expression of countenance.

But William was not to be kept quiet, and he explained—" My dear July, I like to hear a man express his determination to work, and when I am pleased I can't help showing it. I'm sorry if I've vexed the governor, but the truth's the truth, and I must say I think your brother's a brick."

Royle smiled, and thanked him for his sympathy; and Mr. Dawson inquired what form this new-born energy would take.

"Are you thinking of business? going to set up a rival tea-shop?" he asked.

Royle shook his head, saying, "I don't think I should make a good man of business. I want to try something else, but have not yet talked it over with my father."

"Go into business, my dear fellow," urged Dawson; "go into business. Depend upon it, there's nothing like it. If you once succeed, you make money by sackfuls. You have a regular, steady work ready to your hand. It's not necessarily a question of brain—it's more a question of machinery. You churn on at it for years and years—the quality of the labour doesn't matter so much as the quantity; you must keep straight at it, whether or no your arm aches, and you must keep your eyes open, too, to see that none of your business friends come and take your cream; and then, one day, at last the butter comes. If you go into a regular profession, it's one long struggle from beginning to end. You may or may not succeed, according to chance. It's no question of a fair, stipulated amount of work getting a fair, stipulated amount of pay. Then, look at the study you must get through first. No; if I were you I should fix my mind on business."

"I should say," remarked Hester, the eldest daughter of the house, "that Philip ought to discover in what direction his tastes lie. That is the most important thing, isn't it, papa?" she added, appealing to her father.

"I am not going to have anything to

say in the matter," said Mr. Royle. " I shall talk it over with Philip when the time comes, and that will be quite enough of it all for me."

" It would be a pity for you to take up any kind of occupation you didn't like," continued Hester, gravely, addressing herself to her brother. " It makes such a great difference in the success of your work, if you do it with all your heart. Haven't you any particular wish ? "

"I don't see the use of discussing Philip's vocation," said Ellen, authoritatively. " If any man were ever designed for one special thing, I'm sure Philip is cut out for the stage. He delights in elaborate, sensational sort of speeches, and he seems to have been acting to perfection of late, in his fashionable circles of society, and in his home, since he has hoodwinked everybody."

"Oh, Philip, yes," murmured Effie, in a tone of delight. "I would give anything to hear you play Romeo."

A general laugh, in which even Mr. Royle joined, followed this; and Royle himself said, good-humouredly—

"Poor little Effie, you would be terribly disappointed if you did, I should think." Then he added, turning to his sisters, and addressing them in a body, "You need not trouble yourselves to discuss the matter to-night, however. I am sure you must have some local subjects of conversation far more interesting to you, and as my father won't discuss the matter yet, I can say nothing definite."

"Are you going already, Philip?" asked Effie, as her brother rose from his chair, and looked at his watch.

He nodded assent, and stepped across to his father, saying, "Good night, sir; I am sorry that you are so displeased, but I hope that you will alter your mind a little, sooner or later. I shall come up again in a day or two, for I am anxious to have some definite plan."

Mr. Royle grunted an answer, in which the words "high-flown nonsense," and, "the later the better," were heard; and Royle was obliged to be satisfied with his father's abrupt manner and speech. He kissed the bevy of sisters, and turned to William Dawson with a cordial smile and a hearty "Good night." After all, this vulgar soap-boiler had been quick to appreciate his newly-found independence of spirit, and Royle could not but be grateful to him for his sympathy.

"Good night," responded Dawson; adding, with a smile, "I congratulate you, in spite of the governor, and hope you will get on. If ever I can do anything for you, you know where to find me, and I shall always be ready to do the needful for you, to the tune of a fiver, until you are fairly set up. But, I say, remember what I said just now, and stick to business!

"By Jove!" continued Dawson, when Royle had gone, and the family had resumed their usual evening aspect, "there's something in the young man, after all!"

"There's a fine amount too much in

him," said Mr. Royle, severely. "And the result of the whole concern will be that he will marry some drab of a girl, and get into an awful pickle, and I shall have to keep him just as thoroughly as I do now, without any pleasure in it."

"Oh, you governors are terribly put upon, there's no doubt about it," laughed Dawson. "There's one comfort—you have victimized your governors in your time, and it's only fair that your turn should come."

"I hope you will always be as reasonable, that's all I've got to say," remarked Mr. Royle. "And now I must tell you that I am perfectly disgusted with Philip and all his affairs, and I wish you would talk about something else, and drop the subject. Drop it—drop it."

"All right, governor, mum's the word!" cried Dawson, with his ever-ready laugh.

He turned the tone of the conversation by a vigorous onslaught at his future sister-in-law Charlotte, respecting the charms and caprices of the Rev. Augustus Wentworth; and Philip Royle was not mentioned in his father's house for some days.

CHAPTER IX.

THE weeks rolled slowly on, to Royle's mind, after the interview with his father. Most of his friends had gone down to their country-houses for Christmas, and amongst them the Clevedons and Joce-lyn ; so Royle saw very few people indeed during the closing weeks of the old year and the opening weeks of the new year.

Nor was he inclined for much society. He was thinking over the perplexing questions of daily work and daily bread, and did not care to pause in his reflections. He crossed the Park to his father's house several times, with the view of discussing his prospects with his father. But Mr. Royle invariably contrived to say as little as could possibly be said, each time professing to postpone any serious conversation until his son's next visit; and Royle was thoroughly dissatisfied with the existing state of affairs.

He sat in his handsome rooms in Regent Street, evening after evening, revolving his own scheme in his mind, and asking himself how far it could succeed. He knew that the world in which he had lived for so long would 'drop' him for a time; but he also knew that he might win himself a solid place in society, if he succeeded. He knew that society pardons anything in a successful man, and was convinced that the tea-dealing and soap-boiling would be overlooked in a rich and glorious future. But had he the courage, the genius, necessary to the following out of his idea? he asked himself again and again. Could the passing taste be developed into a commanding talent, that would compel the attention of the whole of society? Mere mediocrity would never satisfy him —he must attain pre-eminence; and, though he hardly realized what he wished to do when his honours were full upon him, he was conscious that no small instalment of fame would suffice. Then, at times, it seemed to him absurd quixotism to throw up his present comfortable and easy life, and enter upon a course of arduous exertion. His father did not murmur at his inactivity—his father asked nothing more of him than that he should spend as much money as he wished, and eventually marry a rich wife. Many men, he knew, would be delighted at such a prospect. Why should not he throw over his schemes and theories, and enjoy himself placidly and indolently on the fruits of his father's labour?

He found himself continually pondering and wavering over the question; and at last, one evening, in utter bewilderment at his own contradictory thoughts, he seated himself hurriedly at his writing-table, and wrote a full account of his troubles and ceaseless self-communings to Silvia Clevedon. He hardly knew why he wrote to her. She had never given him permission to address her by letter, and he felt that she would be considerably surprised to hear from him; still an impulse prompted him, and he wrote. When the letter was posted, he regretted his temerity. He tried to remember the literal wording of certain phrases, and he dared not call to mind the number of sheets of letter-paper he had covered. He told himself repeatedly that she would never answer, that she would be irrevocably disgusted with his want of resolution and courage, that she would never wish to know him again; and, as the days flew by, he blamed himself more and more energetically for his folly in writing. Several days passed and left his mind unrelieved.

He watched for his letters at first with

quick, eager eyes and ears; but gradually, as his hopes for a reply faded, he grew graver and more indifferent to the periodical postman's knock, and when he came home in the evening, turned carelessly and indolently to the letters that happened to be lying on his table.

Only those who have waited for a letter at some important moment in their lives can realize the harassing effect of such prolonged expectation — the constant activity and self-delusion of the mind in finding excuses for the writer, in making allowances for the difficulties of transit, in foreseeing every conceivable disaster in the post-office. Royle was singularly anxious to have if only a reassuring word from Silvia Clevedon, and he was inexpressibly worried by the thought, growing gradually more intense, that she was angry at his weakness of resolution, and was also angry at his presuming to write her a long letter. He was astonished to find himself so keen and eager in the matter. It really did not much concern him, he argued, whether or not she were displeased. The loss of her regard would make one pleasant friendship the less—that was all; it was not a question for serious consideration. She had, most probably, forgotten him entirely by this time, and was wondering where she could have met a man bold enough to write to her uninvited. And yet she had been kind and sympathetic to him. He had talked to her of his hopes and prospects in life, as he could have talked to no other girl that he knew; for most young ladies would have gaped in his face at the first sentence. He had found her full of interest and encouragement as to his nascent independence of spirit; in fact, she had been so friendly, so frank, so generous in her sentiments and ideas, that she seemed to him like an ideal woman, unhampered by the petty ill nature and gossip which are the most conspicuous jewels in the crowns of a fair portion of feminine society, and far above all considerations of coquetry. It had never entered Royle's head that many persons might have called his devotion to Miss Clevedon a genuine flirtation, and he had no scruples in absorbing her, in claiming her whole attention when he met her, just as he had had no scruple

in writing to her a frank and fair confession of his wavering thoughts and
fancies. However, as the days went by,
he ceased to hope for an answer to his
appeal, and he did his utmost to forget
the incident, and to resume his self-
communings.

But his reward was coming, and one
evening, when he had been dining at his
father's and reached his rooms at about
ten o'clock, Royle found upon his table
a letter, the envelope of which was
directed in an unknown handwriting.
His face flushed as he caught it up. "It
cannot be from her," he muttered, as he
looked intently at it. Yet the writing
hardly seemed that of a woman. It was
close and compact, without any of the
usual feminine sprawls and flourishes.

"Then she is not like most women," he
said to himself, and he tore open the
envelope with a strange glow of satisfaction, and read the letter by the fireside.

"My dear Mr. Royle" (it ran)—

"I have been long in answering
your letter, but the truth is that it has
puzzled me somewhat. You tell me half
your story, and expect me to advise you,
to pronounce an opinion as to the whole.
I am sorry that, since your confidence
prompted you to write to me, it did not
induce you to tell me *all* your 'vain hopes
and worries.' You know, Tennyson says,
'A lie that is half a truth is ever the
blackest of lies;' and I feel inclined to
make a poor and miserable foot note,
to the effect that a truth that is only

half a truth is a worthless truth, after
all. You tell me your weaknesses and
failings of spirit, your irresolution, your
lack of courage to face the world alone;
you speak of some career in which you
think you might possibly excel; you talk
of dreams of fame, of visions of success
and happiness; you ask for my sympathy
and help; but you say nothing as to the
bent of the profession you think of adopt-
ing. Therefore, how can I give you
advice? We shall be in London shortly,
and when I see you we can talk these
matters over. I am sorry that your
father discourages you in your independence of feeling. I can understand that
he should be disappointed, certainly. He
has had his ideal, and it is hard that his
own son should destroy it. Still, I fancy

that, sooner or later, he will recognize the justice of your views. There is also one further remark that I must make to you. If you do not really feel the independence of spirit which leads a man to prefer to earn his own bread, you had much better leave your lot in your father's hands. When you speak of 'hesitating' and 'wavering,' you make me doubtful of you, for such an effort as yours requires thorough conviction and perfect strength of purpose.

"You ask me what I should do were I in your place. There would be no question in my mind, I assure you. Even as I am, it has often occurred to me that I should be happier and better if I were required to exert myself, in some one way or another, for the benefit of some object or person. My burden of easy idleness is quite as irksome to me as is the burden of labour to many of my fellow-creatures. There is so much to be done in the world, that it seems cruel and unjust that I should be living in luxury, doing nothing, while others are struggling in misery and working hard. Does it never strike you that life is unfair from beginning to end? Do you never feel a kind of compunction for your well-being?

"I know that I should be much happier if I were in your place, free and independent, and working bravely for my own living, and I believe that you, if you take this decisive step, will be happier too. But I am afraid to persuade you— the responsibility is too great. I most heartily wish you every success, however, whatever may be the path you choose, and you will lose no real friends, be assured. When I see you in London, we will, if you like, discuss the career upon which your thoughts are bent.

"Believe me,

Yours faithfully,

"SILVIA CLEVEDON."

As Royle read this characteristic letter, he seemed to hear, as if in a dream, the ceaseless, trivial chatter of his sisters, and the fastness and occasional vulgarity of their conversation came to his mind in vivid contrast to Silvia Clevedon's serious, thoughtful sentences. He put down the long-expected and anxiously awaited letter with a sigh of relief at last. She was neither angry nor disgusted, evidently; she had no idea of dropping him; she was not offended; and a weight was lifted from his spirit as he became convinced of these facts. His gratitude to her for her friendliness was so great, that his first impulse was to write a second and still more confidential letter; but a little consideration showed him that it would be wiser to leave his gratitude unwritten, trusting to an early opportunity of expressing it to her, by word of mouth.

"She is right," he muttered to himself, as he paced up and down the room. "I ought to have a thorough conviction and strength of purpose to help me through. I ought to feel a *feu sacré;* I ought to be certain of myself. But

I want an aim, an object. If I had but some one for whom to work ! "

And, with a feeling of vague discontent, Royle read Miss Clevedon's letter once again, before he put it in his pocket ; and went out to join a friend's supper-party in Maddox Street, with singular disinclination towards festivities of every kind. He was not a convivial guest on this particular occasion, as his companions, with the uncompromising frankness of men towards each other, speedily informed him, and he soon left them and returned to his own rooms, determined to forget his pre-occupations, for a time, in sleep.

CHAPTER X.

ONE grey morning, at the end of February, as Silvia Clevedon and Gilbert Jocelyn were sauntering along the broad paths of the Clevedon House grounds, towards the lodge-keeper's little domain, they heard sounds of human voices at a high pitch, voices that unmistakably belonged to an angry man and a crying woman. Silvia stopped immediately.

"There is something wrong at the lodge," she said.

"Oh, it's only the man and his wife quarrelling," said Jocelyn, impatiently.

"But it's odd if they are quarrelling," said Silvia; "for Johnson is such a good husband, and they are such a happy couple, that, although they have been with us years, I have never heard of them exchanging an angry word. I wonder what is the matter?"

"You will only get yourself insulted if you go and ask," said Jocelyn. "Why can't you leave them to fight it out? What has it all got to do with us? Why shouldn't we have our stroll undisturbed?"

Without heeding Jocelyn's observations, Silvia walked towards the lodge, and was saved the necessity of knocking at the door; for one of the lodge-keeper's children, who had seen her coming, rushed out to catch her hand, and to tell her, between frightened sobs and gasps, that "father was so angry, and mother was crying."

Thereupon Silvia went with the child to the threshold of the modest home, followed by Jocelyn, whose reluctance was overcome by his sense of the duty of protecting Silvia. Silvia looked aghast at the little parlour she had always seen so exquisitely neat and clean. It was littered now with clothes, and sticks, and whips ; a bed had evidently been made up on the sofa that had been the pride of Mrs. Johnson's heart ; some heavy-soled boots were planted on one of her antimacassared chairs ; and the baby was rolling about on the many-hued piece of carpet, and plucking at the fringe on the gaudy tablecloth, with the view of dragging it off the table—an object which was ultimately accomplished, be it noted.

When Silvia appeared at the door, a third child, who had been huddled up in terror in a corner of the room, ran into the kitchen, crying, "Mother, mother, here's Miss Clevedon;" whereupon a gentle-looking little woman, her face all swollen and red with crying, and with the tears still running down her face, came upon the scene, dropping a mild curtsy as she advanced.

"Why, what can be the matter, Mrs. Johnson?" said Silvia, kindly. "Is it anything in which I can help you?"

"No, miss; I don't think so," said the woman, her tears bursting forth anew. "The master is so very hard, I'm afraid it can't be helped."

" The master ? Which master ? " said Silvia. " You don't mean your husband ? "

" Johnson ? He hard ? Lord love ye, miss," explained Mrs. Johnson, wiping her eyes periodically with the corner of her apron, " Johnson's as soft as butter to deal with, and that's why he's got into this scrape. You see, miss, his brother is gone away to America to-day, and he met my husband last night, and he says, ' Come and have a glass with me at the Foresters', just for the sake of old times, and to wish me luck.' And Johnson couldn't say no, and small blame to him there, at any rate ; and he goes and he has a glass all fair and comfortable enough, and then they get talking, and one thing and another, and they

persuaded Johnson to stay longer than
he meant to, and to take a glass or two
extra, just for the sake of his brother's
company, and they certainly was a little
gone. And they met a party of gentlemen
from the Eagle, and they called out—one
of the gents did—that there was the
admiral's lodge-keeper roaring drunk, and
they told the master pretty soon, somehow or other; for he come down here
the first thing this morning, and he says
to Johnson that he won't hear a word of
explanation, but that Johnson must go
directly, and that he shall tell any one
who comes for Johnson's character about
last night. I know, of course, miss, that
Johnson didn't ought to have taken so
many glasses; but he's as soft as butter
to manage, as I said, and considering his

brother was going away and all, and persuaded him, I don't think he was so bad.
And he wasn't roaring drunk, miss, I do
assure you; he was only lively and
stupid-like in his talk. But the master
wouldn't listen to what I said, and
wouldn't hear any explanation. So we
have got to go, and what we shall do I
don't know, for if the master tells folks
Johnson was drunk, he will never get
another place."

"Wouldn't my father let you tell him
what you have just told me?" asked
Silvia, gravely.

"No, miss; he wouldn't hear a word,"
sobbed Mrs. Johnson. "He kept saying
that the fact that Johnson was drunk
was enough for him. Perhaps if you was
to tell him how it happened about John-

son's brother going to America, and that Johnson wasn't really so bad as the gentlemen said, he might alter his mind a bit, miss."

Here a broad-shouldered, stalwart man came forward, with his head thrown back, and a look of pride and indignation on his sunburnt face. "No, missus," said he to his wife, "don't you go asking any one to beg for anything from the master. I've served him well all these years, and if he turns me off just for being wrong once, well, let him. I won't ask him to keep me;" and he glanced half sullenly towards Silvia as he concluded.

"But I think my father ought to know how it happened," said Silvia, her beautiful face glowing with genuine sympathy, "and if you do not tell him yourself, Johnson, I will."

"Thank you, miss," said the man turning round towards Silvia, mollified by the kindness of her tone and the concern that her words implied. "I'd own in a minute that I was wrong. I know I ought to keep sober, above all things, and I'm very sorry indeed about last night, and I don't attempt to say that I wasn't just a bit lively. But if the master treats you like a dog, and won't hear a word you've got to say for yourself, well, I'm not the man to go on my knees to him. No offence to you, miss. I know you ain't hard on us, and that you've got feeling for us work-folk; and if I don't have the opportunity of speaking to you again, I should like to say that I don't forget all your kindness to the little uns and the missus, and many's the time we have given a good cheer for you, and drank your health in a glass of cider, before we went to bed. I was a bit surly just now, perhaps, but I meant no offence to you, miss, and I only wish we working people always had such good friends."

"Well, I shall do my best to make it all right for you," said Silvia, with a smile. "Do you know who were the gentlemen you met coming from the Eagle?"

Johnson flushed, and shifted uneasily from one foot to the other; and his wife exclaimed eagerly—

"The master mentioned Squire Morcambe this morning, miss."

"Oh, very well," said Silvia. "Now, don't cry any more, Mrs. Johnson, there's a good creature; at all events, wait and see if you really have anything to cry for. I dare say my father will make it all right."

And with that she turned back towards the house.

"Why, where are you going, Silvia?" asked Jocelyn, following her.

"I am going to have the horse saddled, while I put on my habit," said Silvia, smiling. "You can ride with me, if you like."

Of course, he did like; and when they were both mounted and off, he asked where Silvia was going, and was told—

"To Squire Morcambe's."

It was not till after dinner that evening that the storm burst. Mrs. Clevedon was lying on the sofa, somewhat unwell—

she had been suffering severely of late from the heart-disease that afflicted her— Jocelyn was smoking, and Silvia was gazing absently into the fire, when the admiral, after contemplating his daughter for a few moments, suddenly exclaimed—

"I hear, Silvia, that you went to Morcambe's house this morning."

Silvia raised her frank eyes to her father's face, and answered immediately, without an instant's evasion, "Yes, father, I did."

"May I ask what motive induced you to go there? You know what a bad reputation the man has—that no lady worthy of the name would be seen within his doors; and yet you boldly go there alone, to interfere in some paltry details about a lodge-keeper."

"I did not go alone, father," said Silvia; "Gilbert was with me. I know Mr. Morcambe's reputation, and was all the more surprised that you took his word as a ground for dismissing poor Johnson."

"I am excessively angry at your visit to him," continued the admiral. "He will go all over Hampshire, relating how Admiral Clevedon's daughter came to see him at his house. He won't enter into the absurd reasons of your visit; he will tell just as much of the truth as he thinks fit, and no more."

"But, father dear, since you have so bad an opinion of him," said Silvia, "why did you believe his story about Johnson being 'roaring drunk' last night? Who is to know that Mr. Morcambe himself was not 'roaring drunk'? I am sure that Mr. Morcambe is far, far less sober than Johnson. In fact, Johnson has only been caught this once 'rather lively,' as his poor little wife says, and it seems to me there was ample excuse for the fault, as far as there ever can be excuse for such a loathsome form of misbehaviour. Was Mr. Morcambe sure of what he said, father ? "

" He came here this afternoon, of course," said the admiral, " to say that he must have made a mistake; that the men were not staggering home ; that doubtless his eyes were dazed by coming from the glare of light in the Eagle coffee-room into the street, and so on. You had been talking to him, and your personal appearance made an effect on him, and he was ready to take any oath in order to please you. But I saw through him in this case, and am not to be hood-winked and wheedled by my daughter's machinations. Johnson shall go. He was seen perfectly tipsy in the High Street by a number of gentlemen, and he shall go."

"And how about the gentlemen, father?" said Silvia. "How many times have they been seen perfectly tipsy, I wonder? And yet they are not punished. The men at the Eagle drink as much as the men at the Foresters'; the only difference is that at the one place they are rich, and at the other they are poor. I am sure you can hardly remember how many times you have heard stories about Mr. Morcambe's dissipation. He has no excuse. He is rich; he can afford to cultivate any taste he may have; he can afford to have friends to see him—to buy books, and pictures, and horses; he can afford to travel if he choose; in fact, he can afford to amuse himself as best he likes, so he spends the greater part of his time in dissipation. Now, even if poor Johnson got tipsy every week, he would have more excuse, for he has nothing better to do with his spare time. He has no tastes for art, for reading, for science, because ever since he was a child he has been hard at work, and has had no time to cultivate anything but muscular strength, and that involuntarily. He has no horse to ride, no trap to drive; he cannot go shooting in the preserves; he cannot even pick an apple in the orchard; he has no possible means of enjoying himself but by drinking and smoking."

"You are talking nonsense, Silvia," said the admiral angrily. "I was not saying anything about Johnson's enjoying himself. I have nothing to do with that. Let him enjoy himself the best way he can; only let him keep himself sober when he is out in the village, so that people are not forced to notice the condition in which my servants are allowed to be."

"But, father," pleaded Silvia, "this is the first time you have found Johnson at fault. Surely you might excuse him for once? Why, he has been with us nine or ten years, and yet you turn him away on so slight a provocation. I suppose Mr. Morcambe told you, as

I told him, how it happened. I assure
you, even Mr. Morcambe seemed impressed."

"What folly!" cried the admiral.
"Why, Silvia, Morcambe told me the
whole ridiculous story, and the only
remark he made was that you had the
brightest eyes he had ever seen."

"If he thought so, why shouldn't he
say so?" said Silvia, imperturbably.
"It's not my fault, father, if I have,
or if I have not, bright eyes. I don't
see that that has anything to do with
the question. However, if you have
really made up your mind that Johnson
is to go, there is nothing to be said—
only the injustice of the thing makes
me quite hot with indignation. You
let Mr. Morcambe come here and see

you continually, and you take his word against an honest man whom you have known for years, and who has now been caught in the wrong for the first time; yet you know that Mr. Morcambe is not to be trusted—that he drinks far more than Johnson could afford to do. It makes me miserable that people who are flesh and blood like ourselves, and who work hard all their lives to earn the money we throw away, should be treated in this manner."

"If you carry your absurd ideas into execution," said the admiral, grimly, "you'll make nice havoc of the money when it comes to you."

"I hope it never will come to me, father," said Silvia, "if you wish me to do such hard things with it." And she glanced towards Gilbert Jocelyn as she spoke, wondering why he did not interfere in the discussion, and little dreaming how that glance would influence her future.

"You had better let the matter drop, Silvia," said her father, authoritatively, and rising, as he spoke, to leave the room. "I will have no tampering with my word. I said Johnson should go, and go he shall, and neither Morcambe's interference nor yours will prevent it. Do you hear me?"

"Yes, father, I hear you," said Silvia, bending her head; and as the admiral strode indignantly from the room, Silvia turned upon Jocelyn, saying, "Well, Gilbert, you have proved yourself a valuable defender of the oppressed.

Have you been asleep, or were you un-
interested ? "

Jocelyn started and looked somewhat
foolish, and muttered at last that he had
not liked to interfere.

"But you heard all that the poor man
and woman said this morning," rejoined
Silvia, her eyes flashing angrily; "you
heard what Mr. Morcambe said to me;
and you have, finally, heard everything
my father said, and have not an observation to offer, not a simple sentence of
regret at the whole thing to make! You
must surely know how highly my father
thinks of you. If you had said only a few
kind words just now for the poor people,
he would have given in. But you do
not say a syllable. My father knows you
were with me through it all, and naturally

thinks you are not on my side of the question. You were calculating, I suppose, how long it would be before you had another dance or another game of billiards, and did not pay much attention to these vulgar details of home life."

"Really, Silvia," explained Jocelyn, wounded at her contemptuous manner, "I did not think much about it all; and if I had interfered, you would have been certain to be displeased, so I thought if I held my tongue you could not blame me very severely."

"I blame you!" exclaimed Silvia. "But what I say does not matter. Did you not feel indignant yourself at the injustice? I didn't want you to interfere for the mere sake of pleasing me. If you felt no inclination to help the people, why, you were right to say nothing; but I don't see how you can be so cold-blooded."

"You see, I am not so rabid on these subjects as you are," said Jocelyn. "The man will find another place soon enough, I've no doubt; at the same time, the admiral was perhaps rather hard."

"Supposing the admiral were to turn all the gentlemen out of his house who take a little too much wine, not once in ten years, but something more like once in ten days," said Silvia, "how many lords of the creation do you think we should have on our visiting list?"

"Well, you certainly would not have your friend Royle, for one," retorted Jocelyn, with a light laugh.

Silvia turned round upon Jocelyn with her haughtiest glance.

" I don't know why you should mention Mr. Royle to me in that special manner, Gilbert," she said. " He is a man of spirit and a man of courage, and I like him for those reasons. But you forget yourself when you insinuate anything more, even by your voice."

" Children, children ! " interposed Mrs. Clevedon, quietly, from the sofa ; " don't talk to each other, since you are both so angry. Wait until you are cool and calm before you discuss the point on which you disagree."

" It is all over now, mother," said Silvia, whose anger was calmed in a moment by her mother's voice ; and she went to sit beside the sofa on which Mrs. Clevedon lay, leaving Jocelyn to read the *Spectator* in uneasy silence.

In a week, before the month required as a warning had expired, Johnson the lodge-keeper, and his wife and children, were turned adrift, in sullen, bitter anger with "the master," and full of regret at leaving the young lady of the house. Johnson's dismissal was a sore point with the admiral ever after; and his daughter's interference, and the high ground she took, never ceased to rankle in his mind.

CHAPTER XI.

EARLY in March, the Clevedons came up to town, to enter upon the duties of the season, and with them came Jocelyn, who hardly seemed to have the strength of will to break away from the thraldom of Silvia's society. He followed her from place to place without knowing exactly why he did so. When she went to Lyndwood, he went down to Lyndwood; when she returned to London, he returned to London; and while the admiral looked on delightedly at what seemed to him the natural development of his pet scheme, Silvia herself did not pay any attention to Jocelyn's devotion, and allowed him to accompany her in her walks and drives, for all the world as if he had been her brother. Indeed, she always thought of him in a sisterly manner, and it never occurred to her that he was more than fraternal in his sentiments.

To Silvia, the opening of the season seemed somewhat dreary. She was sorry to leave Lyndwood, for she had a positive affection for the primitive quiet of the old-fashioned country place. Then, she was afraid that her mother might be considerably wearied and fatigued by the excitements of town; and her father, she knew, was less likely than ever to be

lenient to her in all little social matters, for
he had grown far more stern and rigorous
since the episode of Johnson's dismissal.

"Where are you going, Silvia?" asked
the admiral, as they sat down to dinner,
a few nights after their arrival in London,
in full evening dress. "To a couple of
balls?"

"No, father dear—to the first night
of the season at the opera," said Silvia.
"Mrs. Grey has a ball to-night, and
begged us to go after the opera; but it
would only be fatiguing for mother, and
I'm sure I do not want to go."

"Why, you promised me the first
waltz there," exclaimed Jocelyn, in a
disappointed tone.

"Did I?" said Silvia, carelessly.
"You will have to find another partner

then, for I am not going to drag mother there. I know she doesn't want to go any more than I do."

"You are polite to Gilbert," said the admiral.

Silvia looked at her father in astonishment, and smiled as she answered, "Gilbert knows what I mean. He doesn't expect me to go to Mrs. Grey's for the sole purpose of waltzing with him—do you, Gilbert? Also, I do not care for dancing at all, as a rule."

"Of course, you would not condescend to care for anything that amuses other young people of your age," said the admiral, testily.

"I tell you what it is, though," said Jocelyn, briskly; "it's very pleasant to get back to town, and to see all the men you know, and hear all the news. I couldn't help thinking to-day, as we had our billiards and our bitters, that you might say what you liked about the aspect of nature and all that, but there is nothing like the civilization of town, after all."

"In short, you prefer the green of the billiard-table to the green of nature," said Silvia.

"Well, upon my word, Silvia," said Jocelyn, apologetically, "one is more humanizing than the other. You meet a number of men about the green cloth, and you get sociable and make friends, and you can have your brandy-and-soda or your bitter comfortably, and your amusement is found all ready for you. But I find the green trees very poor company, I must frankly own. Their leaves and branches are pretty enough, I grant, and it's very convenient to get into their shade when the sun is too hot, or when there is a shower of rain. But when you have said that, you have said all. As to their influence— well, it seems to me that their waving and whispering, and all the other wonderful things the poets say they do, is deucedly gloomy."

"Poor Gilbert!" said Silvia, laughing heartily, "you are evidently Amy Leveson's affinity. She believes that Providence has arranged all the garden land of England with a special eye to croquet and lawn tennis."

"The Levesons called here to-day," said Mrs. Clevedon; "they said they should see us to-night at the opera. Lady Leveson asked after you, Gilbert, and Miss Leveson asked particularly after Mr. Royle. His appearance seems to have made an impression upon her."

"What a foolish girl she is!" exclaimed Silvia. "I cannot see what there is to admire ecstatically in Mr. Royle."

"By-the-by," said Jocelyn, glancing furtively at Silvia as he spoke, "it seems that Royle has disappeared from the face of society. All the fellows at the club are wondering what has become of him. His old haunts know him no more, and every one thinks that he must have been doing something shady."

"And yet you men talk about the spitefulness of women!" remarked Silvia.

"But you must own that it's odd," said Jocelyn. "Not only has he not turned up at the club, but he has been absent from the balls and parties that have hitherto taken place. Some one suggested that the mysterious source from which his money is derived had deserted him, and that he dared not show his face *sans le sou;* but I think myself he must have got into some scrape—had a bout of drinking, or lost heavily at cards, or fallen in love under unfortunate circumstances. He was always a wild fellow."

If Jocelyn's remarks were intended to mortify Silvia, they missed their mark, for she did not appear to hear what was being said, and made no answer whatever to his observations. She was wondering what Royle had done—how far he had

carried out his resolutions—if her letter
had decided him in one way or the other.
He had evidently made some change in
his mode of living, since he had given up
his club, and had missed the first balls
of the season.

"Hang the fellow!" muttered Jocelyn
to himself, seeing Silvia's abstraction.
"She's positively quite interested in
him."

In due time the carriage was announced, and Mrs. Clevedon, Silvia, and
Jocelyn were whirled away to the brilliant
opera-house, where they held a miniature
levée between the acts. Silvia noticed,
however, that Royle did not make his
appearance; she did not see him in the
house, and he did not come, as he had
been in the habit of doing, to their box.

At last, when it was all over, and Silvia and Mrs. Clevedon were standing on the last step of the grand staircase, waiting for the carriage to be called, Silvia caught sight of Royle at the entrance to the stalls, talking to one or two gentlemen.

In a moment the men passed on, and Royle, turning round, perceived Silvia's tall, white-robed figure and noble head, her whole form seeming to him to stand out in bold relief among the vapid prettinesses that surrounded her. He sprang forward instantly to greet her, and felt something strange stirring at his heart, as he touched her hand and met her bright smile. Lady Leveson and her daughter stood close by, and as Royle bowed to them, he

devoutly wished them out of his way,
for he guessed that he should be unable
to say a word to Silvia. Jocelyn was
there, too, with several men he knew, and
Royle felt it was hopeless to expect a
possibility of even thanking Miss Clevedon
for her letter.

"Oh, Mr. Royle," cried Amy Leveson,
with her pretty air of simplicity, "I was
told by Mr. Noel that you had abjured
society—that you were going to do something as dreadful as being a monk!"

"Am I?" said Royle, glancing towards
the informant, who was now gossiping
with Jocelyn. "Perhaps Noel can tell
me what form my villainy will take."

"Everybody has been complaining of
you, you know," said Amy Leveson,
coquettishly. "We are all very angry,

for you have not been to see us, and you did not even come and pay your respects to us this evening, as you ought to do."

"I am sorry if I have appeared rude," said Royle, "but the truth is that I have been very much occupied, and have been compelled to neglect many social duties." Here he turned towards Silvia, determined to speak to her, if only to make the usual society remarks, and said, "My occupations have prevented me calling on Mrs. Clevedon also; but I trust she will excuse me."

Mrs. Clevedon smiled; and Silvia said, encouragingly, "Occupation is a good plea, Mr. Royle."

Just at that moment, there was a sudden sway in the great crowd, and a feminine voice was heard to exclaim in tones of unmistakable delight, " Philip ! Philip ! "

Royle turned hastily round, and at the head of the throng of people coming from the pit, he saw his sister Effie, accompanied by his sister Julia and his future brother-in-law, William Dawson. Effie was in bright blue silk, and Julia was in black silk, and both sisters wore the inevitable red opera-cloak ; while William Dawson in evening dress looked, it seemed to Royle, ten times more vulgar than he did in his ordinary daily costume. A man looks either exceptionally well or exceptionally ill in evening dress, and Mr. Dawson was undoubtedly among the least-favoured gentlemen. Altogether, the party of three advancing upon Royle

from the pit, looked as far removed from
the distinguished beauty of Silvia Clevedon, the graceful elegance of Amy Leveson, and the thorough-bred bearing of
Jocelyn, Noel, and others, and of Royle
himself, as members of the one vast
human family could possibly look.

Royle remembered for a very long
time his sensations on the first perception
of the *contretemps*, which rapidly went
the round of his circle of friends, and
was related with chuckles for years afterwards, whenever Royle's name was mentioned. He saw as if in a dream the
brilliant crowd, the handsome staircase
thronged with the wives and daughters
of noble houses, the special group of
so-called friends around him. He saw
Lady Leveson's contemptuous expres-

sion; he saw Amy Leveson hide her face behind her fan; he saw the men look towards each other with a laugh and something like a wink; he saw his youngest sister's pretty face beaming with pleasure at meeting him; he saw Dawson's broad smile and Julia's simper; —but he did not dare glance towards Silvia.

The little group that had been bubbling with laughter a moment before, was suddenly quite silent, while Royle stood perfectly calm and pale at Silvia's side, looking Mr. Dawson full in the face and making no sign.

The position was critical, and the persons not immediately concerned watched its development with evident amusement. At last Mr. Dawson seemed impressed with the idea that his recognition was inopportune, and he turned sharply on his heel, saying, in his usual loud voice, and with his customary bluntness of speech—

"Come along, Eff. You see your brother doesn't want you—he's with his fine friends."

Silvia heard what he said; she saw the change of expression in the younger girl's large blue eyes; and with a reproachful look at Royle, she said, "Will you not introduce your sisters to us, Mr. Royle?"

Royle muttered something totally unintelligible in reply, stepped after Dawson and his sisters, and in a moment had presented them to Mrs. Clevedon and to Silvia, and had heard Silvia say to Effie—

"I have known your brother for some months, and I am sorry I have not happened to meet you before."

For a few seconds, Silvia spoke to Royle's sisters; and Royle could not but notice that Dawson seemed completely awed by her appearance and manner, and did not hazard any vulgar allusion or comic saying, confining himself to a declaration that the heat in the pit was enough to send a fellow into the middle of next week.

At last the cry, "Mrs. Clevedon's carriage stops the way," broke up the group. Jocelyn hurried forward to offer his arm to Mrs. Clevedon, and Silvia, after shaking hands cordially with Effie and Julia, and bestowing a smile and a bow on Dawson, took Royle's arm of her own accord.

"Excuse me," cried Royle to his sisters, and, in a bewildered whirl of mind, he led Silvia to the carriage.

During the moment's pause required for Mrs. Clevedon to be installed in its luxurious depths, Silvia said, gently, "Mr. Royle, I was almost ashamed of you just now."

"One of these days I will make you proud of me!" he answered, raising his head with the dignity of a man who feels he has something great in him.

Silvia had no time for another word; she sprang into the carriage, and it rolled away, and the two men returned to their respective parties.

With the slightest of bows to the Levesons, and Jocelyn, and the group of persons generally, Royle took his sister

Effie's hand, and drew it through his arm. He accompanied Dawson and his sisters to their cab-door, and as he was bidding them "good night," Dawson interrupted him by saying—

"I tell you what it is—that tall girl in white is A 1, and no mistake!"

As Royle paced up and down his room that night, recalling every incident of the evening, he muttered to himself again and again, "I will keep my word. She *shall* be proud of me one day!"

END OF VOL. I.

LONDON: PRINTED BY WILLIAM CLOWES AND SONS, STAMFORD STREET AND CHARING CROSS.

www.ingramcontent.com/pod-product-compliance
Lightning Source LLC
Chambersburg PA
CBHW031421020726
47499CB00005B/1537